It's Too Late for Sorry

Bradbury Press   Scarsdale, New York

IT'S TOO LATE FOR SORRY

A Novel by Emily Hanlon

Library of Congress Cataloging in Publication Data
Hanlon, Emily. It's too late for sorry.
Summary: Fifteen-year-old Kenny's involvement with the mentally retarded youth on his block brings out the best and the worst in him.
[1. Mentally handicapped—Fiction. 2. Friendship—Fiction]
I. Title.
PZ7.H1964It   [Fic]   78-4422
ISBN 0-87888-136-0

For my mother, and for Beth

It's Too Late for Sorry

Chapter 1

I knew Harold had moved into the Harrigans' house, but I hardly gave it a thought. I didn't think I'd have too much in common with a retard.

Phil thought differently. "Hey, Kenny, did you hear you got a retard for a neighbor?" he asked one Monday morning.

"Yeah, I know. My mother told me."

"How come you didn't tell me? I mean, it's not often a real live mental retard moves next door to your best friend."

"First of all, I didn't think it was a momentous occasion. And secondly, he's not my neighbor. The Harrigan house is three houses away."

"Splitting hairs," Phil said sarcastically.

"Okay," I sighed. "The next time a retard moves in on my block I'll send you a telegram."

Phil was annoyed. I could tell by the expression on his face. Ever since school started he'd been like that—touchy over little things, things that hardly seemed to matter, like this retard. One minute he'd look like he wanted to punch me and the next he'd be grinning like nothing happened.

"You don't know what you're missing, Kenny. Pete saw him Saturday morning and he said it was a trip just looking at him. Did you see him yet?"

"No."

"I guess that's why you're not more into the retard."

"Yeah, maybe . . ."

I was about to add, "But I doubt it," when the first bell rang. "I gotta go, Phil," I told him. "I have to finish my geometry homework." I started to leave.

"Kenny," Phil called.

"Yeah."

"Wait till you hear Pete describe the retard. That'll change your mind."

I pushed my way through a mass of kids and hurried up the front steps of school to my homeroom.

At lunch that day I got the whole story on Harold.

"It was Saturday morning," Pete began, "and I was delivering groceries. So anyway, there's this big order to a house on your block, Kenny. I'd never delivered there before. An old lady answers the door and she tells me to bring the packages into the kitchen. So I do. And there's this kid sitting at the kitchen table, staring at a peanut butter and jelly sandwich. Well, he wasn't really a kid. I guess he's about our age. But right away I knew there was something wrong with him because nobody stares at a peanut butter and jelly sandwich!" He laughed. Phil did, too. They were both beginning to crack up.

I looked at Al and Greg, who were sitting at the table, too; and the three of us began to grin. Pete and Phil were getting hysterical.

"Go on. Tell him how he looked," Phil urged.

"Weird." Pete laughed. "Really weird. I couldn't help staring at him and believe me I was trying not to because I can get a big tip on orders like this. But I couldn't help it. I've never seen a face like that!"

"Gross?" Phil asked.

"You might say that, Phil. You might say that! And then all of a sudden the kid looks up at me and grins. For no reason. I mean, I definitely didn't talk to him. He looks at me and grins. Man, you should have seen his teeth—rotten to the core. And it looked like he had two sets of them. I swear!" Pete laughed. And he laughed and laughed. So did Phil. They were laughing so hard they couldn't even talk. Greg and Al and I were laughing, too—I think more at Pete and Phil than at the retard story. Their laughter was catching.

"Tell them what happened next," Phil gasped.

"Okay, okay," Pete said, trying to stop laughing. Finally he just blurted out, "The kid talks! He says, 'My name's Harold.' But you had to hear him to believe him. Weird. That's when I knew he was retarded."

We all laughed about the retard during lunch and Phil did an imitation of what he thought a retard would look like. It was funny, but I didn't think any more about it until Phil called later on that night.

"I'd really like to see the retard," he said.

"Yeah?"

"Don't you?"

"Not much."

"But he lives right down the street from you! Aren't you interested?"

"I guess if I saw him, I'd look."

"What's the matter with you, Kenny? You used to always be up for something like this."

3

"A retard?"

"Think of the possibilities, man. I mean, a retard could be lots of laughs. Remember crazy Joe, who used to clean up the parks? He was probably a retard all along except we never realized it!"

Phil and I had really done a number on crazy Joe three summers ago. Joe would walk around with one of those pointed sticks, harpooning garbage and shoving it into an old burlap bag he carried on his shoulder. Phil and I would follow him around, dropping pieces of paper behind him. Then we'd run to him and point out all he'd missed. Joe never once caught on to us. He'd just shake his head, stare at the garbage we'd dropped, and pick it all up.

The funniest thing we did to him was when Phil pulled the string at the bottom of his burlap bag. The whole bottom ripped open. Joe didn't realize it. He just kept on walking along, his head bent, his eyes glued to the ground, jabbing the garbage and shoving it into the burlap bag. Usually he dragged the bag along the ground so the garbage dribbled out; but every so often Joe would adjust it on his shoulder and lift it off the ground—that's when everything fell out! It must have taken him an hour to realize there was a hole in the bottom. And all the time Phil and I were walking along beside him.

"Poor crazy Joe." I laughed. "We probably drove him nuts."

"Come on! He loved us," Phil insisted. "Nobody paid him more attention than you and me. He thought we were his best friends. Anyway, I was thinking, since you live so close to this mental retard, you could keep your eye out for him. Maybe he's got a routine or something we can pick up on."

I could tell Phil was on one of his jags. I guess he's what you call obsessive—an obsessive nut, but a funny obsessive nut . . .

Staking out a retard wasn't my thing and I didn't really think it was Phil's either, but I agreed to watch out for him anyway.

Whenever I passed I'd look to see if the retard was around. I never saw him; still Phil asked me about him every day.

Friday afternoon Phil told me he was going to hang around Harold's on Saturday morning. "Want to come?" he asked.

"I got football practice," I reminded him.

"I forgot."

So I was surprised when he came over about eight-thirty on Saturday. Practice was at nine.

He walked in through the kitchen door. "Hi, Mrs. Shea!" He grinned at my mother. "Morning, Mr. Shea," he added.

"Morning, Phil," my father muttered, and went back to his paper.

My mother looked up from her magazine and coffee and nodded at Phil. I could hear her sigh under her breath. She doesn't like Phil too much.

Phil sat down at the table and started helping himself to my toast.

Before he even had it off the plate my mother told him, "There's bread in the refrigerator, Phil. Kenny has football practice and he needs his breakfast."

It was my mother's attitude toward Phil that annoyed me. My father didn't ignore him any more than he ignored any of my friends. My mother actively disliked Phil, almost as much as my sister, Patty, did. But Patty's only nine and her opinion doesn't count for much—my mother's does. I don't like all her friends, either, but the roof would fall in if I ever acted toward them the way she acted to Phil. Besides, Phil and I had been friends since fourth grade. You'd think in six years she would have learned to like him. Her attitude never seemed to bother Phil, though. He knew how she felt. Phil's no dope. But he always went out of his way to be friendly. I think my mother posed some kind of challenge to his ego.

"Gee, thanks, Mrs. Shea!" he exclaimed, like she'd offered to make him bacon and eggs. "My mother went away on Wednesday and Perry and I have cleaned out the food."

I don't know if Phil knew that his semi-orphaned state was the one thing that softened my mother's heart toward him. I think he sensed it even though he never said so because he always found a way of letting her know when his mother was away. His mother is a photographer and she travels all over the world on magazine assignments. His father's not home much, either. He's always traveling on business, too; except his mother and father hardly ever travel together. Phil and Perry, his older brother, used to have babysitters, but now they take care of themselves.

"Why didn't you tell me that, Phil?" my mother said to him in a sweeter tone. "Is your father away, too?"

"Thank God," Phil moaned.

My father chuckled. "Always nice to hear a son talk

6

so fondly about his father. That the way you talk about me, Kenny?"

"You never go away," I reminded him.

"True, true." He laughed and went back to his paper.

My mother looked at Phil and shook her head sadly. "Well, you're welcome to eat here any time they're away, you know. Tell Perry he can come, too."

"Thanks, Mrs. Shea."

"Hey, I gotta hurry," I told them. "Grab something from the refrigerator if you're hungry, Phil. Did you ride?"

"Yeah, the bike's outside. I'll ride you to the field."

As soon as we were outside, Phil grabbed hold of me. "I saw him, Kenny! And he's fantastic!"

"Who?"

"Harold. The mental retard!"

"That's great, Phil. But I gotta hurry or I'll be late for practice."

"Come on, Kenny. You got time to stop and see The Mental."

I looked at my watch. I didn't have the time.

"What's a little football practice when it comes to a mental?" Phil laughed, but there was something threatening about the way he laughed, like he was daring me not to go with him.

"Okay. But just for a minute," I said, as I got on my bike.

I didn't go with him because of the dare and I didn't go to see the retard. I went with him because we'd been friends since fourth grade and that's a long time to be friends with someone.

Chapter 2

I couldn't see Harold until we were right in front of the house. He was sitting on the porch steps, sitting and staring, with his crazy mixed-up face pointing up at the sky. I looked to see what he was looking at, but there was nothing there. Not a bird. Not a branch of a tree. Nothing.

Phil nudged me and laughed. "Weird, huh?"

"He's strange," I admitted. I'd never seen a retard before.

"Strange is not the word, Kenny, boy. Martian? Or gross? Maybe like Frankenstein's monster? No, I have it! Ghoulish. The retard's really a ghoul disguised as a human!"

"Keep your voice down, Phil. I don't think this kid lives here alone."

"Don't sweat it." Phil laughed. "I must have been here for twenty minutes before and I didn't see anyone. Look at it this way: if you had a ghoul living in your house, a relative-ghoul, and you saw an honest-to-goodness human being talking to him, would you come out and admit the ghoul belonged to you?"

I shrugged.

"Come on, Kenny, we've been waiting a week to catch a glimpse of the retard and the best you can do is shrug?"

"What am I supposed to do?"

"Wait a minute. I know what's wrong. It's because you haven't seen The Mental in action. He's even better than Pete described."

Phil turned to Harold, grinning like an idiot, and shouted, "Harold! Hiya, Harold! Come here, Harold. Come here, boy!"—just like he was calling a dog.

Harold looked down from the sky and smiled at us. He waved and Phil waved back.

"Wave, Kenny," Phil urged. "We don't want The Mental here to think you're being unneighborly."

I waved.

Harold waved to me and grinned.

I waved again. So did Phil. The three of us were waving back and forth like a retarded brigade. It was pretty funny. The three of us waving and laughing.

"Come on, Harold, old boy, old Mental. Come on over to your pal, Phil!"

Harold pushed himself up like it was a real effort to move and be began walking down the stairs slowly, like a robot. Stiff and robotlike. He was taller than I thought. About as tall as me, about five-nine or so, and big. Not really fat but flabby and out of shape. It was hard to tell how old he was. He could have been sixteen and he could have been thirty.

It was amazing, but once Harold got down the stairs, he moved quickly.

"Guess somebody pushed the fast-forward button!" Phil said.

That was a perfect description. I broke out laughing.

Harold looked like a speeded-up robot. "This is my

new house!" he shouted. He didn't have to, because we were only about four feet away, but he shouted anyway. I thought he was shouting because he was happy. He looked happy. But later on I found out he always shouted. He could hardly talk without shouting.

He walked right up to me and said, "My name's Harold. What's yours?" Then he held out his hand for me to shake.

"Hiya, Harold. My name's Kenny." I shook his hand. Harold grinned and grinned. The more he grinned, the harder he shook my hand, and the harder he shook my hand, the more he grinned. Finally, I pulled loose. Harold looked at Phil and held out his hand to shake.

"I remember you. You Phil," he said.

Phil jumped back as if Harold was poison, and laughed. "I ain't touching him. Maybe the retard's catching."

Harold looked confused, so I put out my hand to shake again. His face lit up. I think shaking my hand was the biggest thrill since his new house.

"It's not so bad," I said to Phil. "The guy just likes to shake hands."

"Your funeral, pal." Phil laughed.

I looked at Harold to see if he understood what Phil meant, but he was still grinning away.

"You don't have to be so hard on him," I said to Phil.

"Hard? Come on, Kenny, where's your sense of humor? He's a moron. He doesn't understand."

"You don't know that . . ."

10

"Yeah, I know that," Phil told me angrily.

I decided to let the matter drop. I could tell Phil was really up on goofing around with Harold. And when Phil's up on something, there's no point in trying to convince him otherwise. I know from experience. Besides, I had to get to football practice. So I said to Harold, "It's real nice meeting you. We're neighbors. I live just down the street."

"Neighbors!" Harold screeched with joy. "I like you, Kenny!" Then he grabbed my hand again and began shaking it like crazy. "Kenneee! Kenneee! See my new house!"

"Listen to the way the jerk talks." Phil laughed. "He sounds like a baby."

"Me no baby. It not nice to call me baby," Harold said. His happy smile vanished as quickly as it came, and his mouth curved down like I'd never seen anyone's mouth curve—except maybe a clown's. I mean, Pete was right, Harold had the weirdest face. Or at least I thought so at the time. Later on I got used to it and it didn't look so bad. Actually, I think it improved, but at first I thought it was weird. You might say his face is double-jointed. He can do anything with it. Anyway, when he looked sad, he really looked sad.

"Cut it out, Phil. He does understand. Can't you see you're hurting his feelings?"

"What do you mean, 'feelings'? He's a mental. A mental doesn't have feelings. He doesn't even know what I'm talking about. Right, retard?" he said, turning to Harold and grinning. It was a mean grin.

Harold looked confused again.

So Phil began shaking his head up and down and grinning, pretending to be friendly. "Right, retard? Right? A mental doesn't know what I'm talking about." And he began laughing like he'd just told the funniest joke in the world. Harold began laughing, too; but the whole thing was definitely turning me off.

"I gotta go, Phil," I said.

"Yeah, I know. Football practice. Gotta get in shape for the big game next week," he shot back.

"That's the way it goes," I sighed.

"Think you're really gonna get to play?"

"Maybe."

"Aw, it doesn't matter to you anyway, does it, Kenny, baby? It's the school spirit that matters— right?"

"Knock it off, Phil. What's the point . . ."

"You're right, Kenny. What's the point?" He turned to Harold. "Do you know what the point is, Mental? I mean, do you know what's the point of spending your Saturdays playing football when you could be hanging out with groovy guys like you and me, Harold?"

"Come on, Phil . . ." I began.

He looked at his watch. "You better be on your way, little boy. Don't want to make the coachie-poo mad at you."

I got on my bike and left.

Chapter 3

Phil *knew* I had football practice. He knew I couldn't have cared less about standing around and making fun of a retarded kid. He knew I wasn't going to miss practice. So why push the point? It's like he was setting me up.

I was pedaling fast, thinking. I know Phil's screwy and unpredictable. Arguing with him is like saying hello. I expect it; but it's never been serious arguing until lately. Like this thing with Harold. What had just happened was typical of the way Phil had been acting since school started.

Here we are, finally, in high school. It may not be the greatest thing in the world, but it's better than junior high, that's for sure. There are things happening here, things you just don't have in junior high, things I really want to do. Like football. I mean I've wanted to make the team more than anything in my whole life. Phil knew it. He's known it for years. It's been a dream since I was in seventh grade. We've talked about it. Sports aren't Phil's thing, but a dream is something you share with your best friend. And he shared his with me, too. I was going to play for the New York Giants and he was going to be an international reporter for *The New York Times*.

So when I first told him I was nervous about the tryouts, I was speechless when he snickered, "You're not
really trying out for the team?"

"Are you nuts? Of course I am."

"Hey, man, dreaming about being a running back
for the Giants is one thing, but spending your life
practicing for some stupid high school team . . ."

"What the hell are you talking about, Phil?"

"I'm talking about you and me and the next three
years. I mean, look at Perry and his friends. You don't
see any of them racing around a football field. And
they're big men around here. I mean, Perry can get
anyone to do anything for him and he's never so much
as joined one crummy club in three years."

Perry's a senior and I get along with him okay. He's
been helpful to Phil and me, introducing us to kids,
telling us which teachers to avoid, things like that.
Sometimes he gives me a lift home. In some ways Perry
and Phil are alike. They're both smart. Phil can get
an A without trying and Perry can, too. Perry wants
to go to Harvard and he'll probably get in.

But there are lots of differences between Phil and
Perry, too, which is lucky because I don't think I could
ever be friends with someone like Perry. He's so cool
he makes me nervous. He's got a certain kind of class,
like he's messy without being a slob. He works at being
messy. Phil and I are just natural-born slobs. Perry is
tall and slim and good-looking. He looks like the guys
in the cigarette ads. Phil is tall and skinny, and I think
he looks all right until you see him next to Perry; then
it's obvious who got all the good looks in the family.
And like Phil says, Perry's popular without joining

14

anything. He always has a girl and he hardly goes out with the same one more than a few times. Even his car says something. It's a 1958 Chevy that he bought cheap and fixed up so it looks like a vintage model.

Perry's always acted okay toward Phil and me; but Phil was never too big on Perry before we got to high school. Phil always used to put his brother down. Suddenly, when September rolled around Perry became some kind of idol for Phil. He acts like riding around in Perry's car and hanging out with Perry and his friends is the only thing to do.

Anyway, when Phil said that to me about trying out for the football team, I just looked at him and sighed. "I don't know what I've been talking to you about for the last two years if it isn't trying out for the team. What about you? The newspaper? I thought you were going to be the editor by the time you were a junior."

I hadn't meant that to come out sarcastically, but it did. Phil glared at me for a few seconds and laughed. "Yeah, I went to the first meeting. They're a bunch of morons. You don't think I'm going to waste my talent on some high school rag!"

"Sorry, Phil, I misunderstood you. I thought you were serious."

"Yeah, and I misunderstood you. I suppose you'll be ass-kissing for a varsity letter next."

I walked away then. My stomach was upset enough thinking about the tryouts. I put the fight with Phil out of my mind. And then after the tryouts, I was riding so high I couldn't think of anything besides what coach Franklin had said.

"You're good, Kenny." He smiled, clapping me on

the back. "But don't let it go to your head. I think you've got the making of a good player if you work at it."

"Then I made the team?"

The coach shook his head and laughed. "You made it, Shea—but I want you to remember one thing: making the team is just the beginning. You won't get to play in one game, no matter how good you are, unless you work. And I mean work. Baldwin's got a record to keep up and we don't keep it up by sitting on our butts. I mean you don't miss one practice unless you've got a damned good reason."

Then he called over one of the other guys. "Chuck, this is Kenny Shea. Kenny, Chuck Simon."

I knew Chuck. Everybody knew Chuck. He was the quarterback.

"Hi." Chuck nodded.

"Did you see this kid play?" the coach asked him.

"Yup."

"What did ya think?"

"He looks okay, coach," he said dryly.

"I think he looks a lot better than okay." The coach grinned.

Chuck looked at me and laughed. "If the coach says so, I guess it's true."

"But I want you to tell him what it's like, being on my team, Chuck."

Chuck pushed his fingers through his hair and sighed. "Tough, Kenny. The coach here is a killer. I mean, if you join the team, it's like signing yourself up for three years of slave labor."

16

"Got the picture, Shea?" the coach said, trying to sound tough.

I nodded.

"Fill him in, Chuck. I got some other kids to see."

When he was gone, Chuck laughed. "That's all a put-on, Kenny. He did the same thing to me when I made the team—got some senior to give me the once-over."

"That's okay. I understand. I like the coach."

"You better." He laughed. "Because if you don't you can't play on his team. Because when you think you've never hated anyone in your whole life as much as you hate that guy—you gotta remember you really love him. He doesn't talk to all the guys the way he talked to you. He really thinks you got potential and that means he'll push you more than a lot of the other kids."

I stood there trying not to grin too much. I felt like I was walking on air.

Somebody called Chuck and he said, "I gotta go. See you around."

"Yeah."

"You know, working with the coach is the best thing that'll ever happen to you at Baldwin, if playing football is what you want to do," he said.

"That's what I want to do," I assured him.

"I'll remind you of that in a month!" Chuck laughed.

Once football started I hardly had time to do anything but practice, eat, and try to do some homework before I fell asleep. There was practice every day from three to five and after the first week the only thing that kept me from total collapse was the fact that I was on the starting team for the first game. I think it was because Bob Kowalski, the split end, pulled a muscle; but that didn't matter.

The Saturday morning that Phil introduced me to Harold was the Saturday before the first game. Thanks to Phil, I got to practice late. When the coach saw me, he looked like he wanted to pull me apart. I was really scared. He began yelling and screaming like a madman, in front of the whole team, about how some snotty sophomore like Shea thought he had it made because a real player like Kowalski got hurt. He ranted and raged for at least five minutes. The rest of the guys were eating it up, especially the other sophomores who were jealous as hell of me. And then the coach made me run up and down the field five times with all my gear on and, in general, terrorized me the whole day. I couldn't do a thing right. He made us rerun patterns a half-dozen more times than usual because of something he said I'd done wrong. By the time practice was over, nobody was gloating anymore—the rest of the guys were ready to kill me!

Chapter 4

I didn't see Phil much the next week. We passed each other in the halls and we had a few classes together, but I got the distinct feeling he was avoiding me. I was so involved with football that I didn't let it bother me. I didn't even have lunch at the same table with Phil and the other guys that week. I sat with some of the other members of the team and we talked over patterns and strategies.

Maybe I was snubbing Phil more than he was avoiding me. I think that's what he thought. On Thursday he was waiting for me outside the lunchroom.

"Hey, Kenny, long time no talk," he said, putting up his arm to stop me.

I didn't know if he was sincere or just setting me up, so I said cautiously, "Sorry about that. I've been busy."

"So I've noticed. You're in the big time now!"

He was shouting to draw other kids' attention. I felt like telling him to shove it.

He went on in the same loud voice. "Care to eat with me? Or is it beneath the dignity of a football player to eat with a mere member of the student body?"

I glared at him for a few seconds and then the stupidity of the whole situation hit me. I began to laugh. "Hey, Phil. This is stupid."

"Your stupidity. Not mine."

I've never known Phil to admit he was wrong about anything and I knew he wasn't about to start now, so I said, "Okay, it's mine. Let's forget it. I've been so involved with the football—yeah, I'd like to eat with a mere member of the student body."

Phil smiled, despite himself. We made our way to the usual table where Al, Pete, Greg, and Herbie were already sitting. Everyone's okay except Herbie. He's been trying to attach himself to Phil and me for years and he's a nerd. He's totally oblivious of the fact that Phil and I can't stand him. We've told him as much, but it doesn't seem to make an impression.

"Welcome home!" Al said, when he saw me.

"It's our long-lost friend!" Greg jeered.

If Phil wasn't the only one who thought I was snubbing him, I figured I had been wrong. "Is it that bad?" I asked, feeling like a fool.

"No worse than any of us would be, I guess." Al laughed.

I began to blush. The put-downs kept on coming for a few minutes, about my head swelling to the shape of a football, and remarks like that. But underneath it all, I had the feeling that the guys were really happy for me, everyone except Phil. He didn't add one witticism to the let's-cut-Kenny-down-to-size free-for-all; and if nothing else, Phil is noted for his witticisms. I figured he was saving them for another time.

Then Herbie chimed in. "Hey, Phil, do one of your imitations for Kenny."

"Aw, come on," Pete sighed. "Give us a break, Herbie . . ."

Phil turned on Pete. "Listen, Farrar, nobody's begging you to sit here. If you don't like the entertainment—leave."

"Okay, Phil," Pete answered quickly. "I didn't mean anything personal. But we've all heard your mental imitations for a week."

"I like them, Phil," Herbie chimed in.

"You mind, Greg?" Phil demanded.

"Who me?" Greg shrugged. "I don't care."

"I'm with Pete," Al said. "I could live without another imitation."

"Then leave. You and Pete leave, because I ain't," Phil shot back.

Pete and Al looked at me like Phil had flipped out.

Al said to me, "It's been like this all week, ever since he met that retard."

"Yeah, I'm beginning to wish I'd never made that delivery," Pete added. "Let me tell you, Kenny, you haven't missed much this week . . . ."

Suddenly Phil grabbed hold of Pete's arm and bent it back. "Hey, man, I don't let anyone talk to me like that."

Pete flung his arm forward. "Don't ever touch me like that again, Canady, or I'll break you in half."

"Come on, guys . . ." I began.

In an instant, Phil was up. He grabbed his books and left the lunchroom. I got up to follow him. So did Herbie.

"Get lost, Holloway," I shouted, and followed Phil. I caught up with him outside the cafeteria. "Wait up, Phil. What's all this about?"

"They're a bunch of retards, all of them—except

21

maybe Herbie. In the long run, maybe he's not so bad."
Phil laughed.

"Why the temper? Pete didn't mean anything . . ."

"I could care less what he meant. And why don't you leave me alone? Go back to your football fantasies." He started to walk away again.

"Wait up, Phil. Let's talk."

"What's to talk about?"

"I don't know. Whatever's bugging you."

"Yeah, I'll tell you what's bugging me. This place is bugging me. High school! It sucks, man. I'd rather spend my time with The Mental than a bunch of high school boobs running around chasing footballs, joining clubs. The whole school spirit—rah, rah! You know something? I hope Baldwin loses on Saturday. I hope you get your asses handed to you."

Phil left and this time I didn't follow. I went back to the lunchroom.

"What's happening?" I asked.

"I don't know," Al began. "It started on Monday. He came in with this imitation of that retard Pete saw. Anyway, he was pretty funny. You know Phil's imitations. He was good. We all cracked up. But he's kept it up all week. It's getting to be a drag. He's got something for this retard and it's making him screwy. I think he goes and sees him every day after school."

"You're kidding!" I exclaimed. "What does he do with him? I mean, I saw the kid. He's pretty retarded."

Al shrugged. "Ask Herbie. I think he's gone with him a few times."

I had a sick feeling in the pit of my stomach. Phil

22

hanging out with Herbie Holloway. "I don't believe it," I groaned.

"It's true," Pete added. "He's tried to get us all to go, but I got better things to do than hang out with a retard."

I went to find Herbie, but I couldn't. I think that he took me literally when I told him to get lost. I bumped into him in between classes later on in the afternoon.

"Hey, Herbie," I called. "I'm sorry I got so mad at you before."

Herbie smiled. "That's okay, Kenny."

"Yeah, well anyway, Al said you and Phil go and visit the retarded kid sometimes."

Herbie giggled, the way only Herbie can. "Yeah. You oughta come sometime, Kenny. I bet it beats football."

"I bet," I sighed.

I think Herbie believed me because then he said, "Phil and me are going after school today. If I tell him you want to come, I bet he'll let you."

"Thanks loads, Herbie, but I got practice. But tell me, what do you and Phil do with Harold?"

Herbie grinned again and began, "See, The Mental is usually sitting on the front steps, like he's waiting for us. He sits there with a pile of rocks, piling them up. Then Phil says, 'Those are really nice rocks you got, Mental.' That's what we call him, The Mental. And then The Mental says, 'I like rocks. You like rocks, Phil?'

"So Phil says, 'Yeah, I love them.' And then he usually falls all over the rock pile. It's real funny, Kenny, because The Mental has this special way of building his rock pile. It's real neat and it always looks the same. At first The Mental almost cried when Phil knocked over the rocks. But now he just laughs, like a little kid with blocks."

"Is that all you do?"

"Oh, no. Phil's real great with The Mental. He talks to him and makes him laugh. You really should come."

"Yeah, maybe I will someday. It sounds like a whole bunch of fun," I said sarcastically.

Sarcasm is beyond Herbie.

He smiled and said, "I'll tell Phil."

"Do that," I said, and hurried to my next class.

Chapter 5

Maybe I shouldn't have, but I put the whole thing with Phil and Harold out of my mind again. There was the game on Saturday, the first game of the year, and for the moment, that was the most important thing. The game was fantastic. We smashed Lakeland 24 to 3. I ran a couple of good patterns and I felt great about the whole game. We all played well.

That night the coach threw a victory party at his house for the team, the band, the cheerleaders, and anyone else we wanted to bring. Everyone had to chip in a dollar. I invited Al and Pete to come. I thought of asking Phil, but I figured there wasn't much point to it.

The party was a blast. The coach plays the guitar and he plays well. He sings, too. He said he used to be in a rock group in high school. It's hard to imagine the coach singing in a rock group, but Chuck told me he's only thirty. His wife is nice. She sang with him and she'd made lots of fantastic food. Everybody had a great time. We were all high on victory.

Chuck offered to drive Al, Pete, and me home. It gets to be a drag having to leave a party when it's convenient for your parents to pick you up. He dropped off Pete and Al first. "Mind if I pick up my sister before I drive you home?" he asked me. "She's babysitting for Mrs. Angelino. Know her?"

"No. I didn't even know you had a sister."

"No kidding. She's a sophomore, too. Rachel."

"I guess our paths just haven't crossed. Is that good or bad?"

"That's hard to tell. Who's objective about sisters?"

"Not me. My sister is a royal pain. But she's only nine."

"Rachel's okay. We get along pretty well. Anyway, Mrs. Angelino is divorced and it's hard for her to drive a babysitter home, so when Rachel babysits, I usually pick her up."

"No sweat. I'm in no hurry. I wish this day could go on forever."

"Yeah, it was great!"

Chuck got out of the car to get Rachel. They were back in a minute. I got out so she could sit in the middle.

"Rachel, Kenny Shea," Chuck said.

"Hi, Kenny!" She smiled. "Good party?"

"The usual—great," Chuck told her. "I keep on telling her she should come to one of the coach's parties but she's too stuck-up."

"That's not true, Chuck," she said indignantly. "But I'm not going to turn down a good-paying babysitting job for a party."

"I can't understand her. Here she can go to one of the most elite happenings of the year and she turns it down for money."

"If you call football elite," she shot back. "Nothing

personal, Kenny, but I think it's you guys on the football team who are stuck-up. The football hero mystique," she sighed. "But I live with one so I know there's no mystique about them!"

"She's an intellectual, Kenny," Chuck countered. "You know, fancy words like mystique. Very psychologically oriented. I think Rachel should be a shrink when she grows up."

"Oh, shut up, Chuck. And I'm not an intellectual, either," she told me. "I'm nothing. I'm just me. I'm too young to *be* anything and I like it that way."

"She's a freethinker. Very big on women's rights," Chuck went on.

"I have to be, in our household. My brother thinks that the world should bow three times a day to the place where the quarterback of Baldwin High lives."

We had to drive through town to get to my house. It was just past eleven and the pizza store was still open.

"Let's stop," Rachel suggested. "I'm starved. Mrs. Angelino never has any good food."

"Okay, but no treating," Chuck said, as he turned into the parking lot.

"The thought never crossed my mind," she said in mock amazement. "It would be a waste of brainpower to even consider such a thing."

"Don't believe her, Kenny. She's always out for a freebie."

"Oh, God," she moaned. "Come on, I'll treat you to a soda."

"What about Kenny?" he asked.

"Hey, no, that's okay. I have money."

"It's the least she can do for the last of the great warriors."

"The last of the great what!" she shrieked.

"Warriors. Well, isn't that what we are, Kenny? Warriors on the great field of football. She thinks it's all fun and games. But when number 22 started coming at me today . . ."

"You mean that huge guy?" I asked.

"The one who looked like King Kong."

"Yeah." I laughed.

"Okay, I'll treat on one condition—no football talk," Rachel said.

"That may be an impossibility," Chuck said.

"Well, try—for the sake of my sanity." She laughed.

I couldn't believe I'd never noticed Rachel before because she really made an impression on me that night. It wasn't so much the way she looked. She's not the most beautiful girl I've ever seen. It's how she looks when she starts to talk. She laughs a lot but she's not silly. She's funny and intense, and her face reflects what she's saying. I usually feel awkward with girls, but I didn't feel that way with Rachel. Maybe it was because Chuck was there and she and Chuck got along so well. We sat and talked and laughed for about an hour until Nino finally closed the store. Then Chuck drove me home.

My mother was still up when I got there. She always waits up for me, pretending to be reading a great book, but I know she's waiting.

"Have fun?" she asked, and then she hugged me.

"Your father and I were both proud of you today. You really looked like a professional out on the field."

"It's just the shoulder pads!" I laughed, and then said, "But what a day, Mom. What a fantastic day!"

"I haven't heard you so enthusiastic about anything in months, Kenny."

"I haven't been."

"I'm glad, really glad. The football is just what you needed. Are you hungry? Patty made a cake."

"Not for one of her cakes." I laughed.

"I helped."

"Still, I'm not hungry. There was fantastic food at the party and then we stopped at Nino's. But I could use something to drink."

My mother and I went into the kitchen and I got a soda and then we began to talk. We talked until one-thirty in the morning. It's not that it's unusual for my mother and me to talk, it's what we talked about. I told her about the party and the coach. She even listened to a play-by-play description of the game. Then, I can't remember how it started, but all of a sudden I was telling her about Phil and me and this thing with Harold. She didn't say much at first. She sat and listened. My mother's a great listener. I could never have told my father all the things I told her that night. He just would never have the time to sit and listen.

After I finished, she said, "It's sick what Phil's doing with that poor retarded boy."

"I know, but the kid probably doesn't know it. I'm more worried about Phil. I know you don't like him, but we've been friends for a long time."

"It's not that I don't like him, Kenny. I've just never thought he was good for you."

"Come on, Mom, all kids do the kinds of things Phil and I did."

Phil and I were always getting into trouble for dumb things like shooting out streetlights with a BB gun, letting the air out of tires, dumping a container of milk into the heating duct at school so that the whole place smelled putrid. My mother always blamed Phil for these things, but it was both of us. Anyway, we'd stopped doing things like that.

"It's not what you did," she went on, "it was your attitude. Phil's attitude. Nothing matters to him. He's so angry at the world and he's trying to make you angry, too."

"That's not true, Mom. Phil and I had more laughs than anybody I know."

"Then how come I haven't seen you as happy as you were when you came in tonight after all those times you and Phil have gone out?"

"That's not the point. The point is Phil. He's my friend and he's getting all messed up. I gotta do something."

"What? Give up football?—because that's what he wants you to do. That'll make him happy—so you'll both be bored and miserable together. Like this summer. The two of you acted like zombies, just because Phil didn't want to do anything . . ."

"Okay, okay, Mom, I know how you feel about all that."

"And your father," she interrupted. "He's just as concerned about your relationship with Phil."

Suddenly I felt angry, more at myself than at my mother. I shouldn't have told her about Phil. I should have known she wouldn't understand.

"Fine—so now I know how you both feel," I told her.

"You're angry now," she said.

"I'm not angry," I insisted.

"What did you want, Kenny? Just for me to agree with you and tell you to wallow in some kind of guilt over Phil?"

"God, Mom, that's not what I want! I just thought that maybe you'd understand about Phil, but that was stupid of me."

"I do understand. It's you who doesn't. You've tried to help Phil and he's let you know in no uncertain terms he doesn't want your help—only your companionship in boredom. Think about it, Kenny. Think about it without getting angry at me."

"Yeah, okay," I sighed.

Then she got up and kissed me "I'm always ready to talk when you want to." She smiled.

"I know, Mom. I think I'll have to work this out myself. Goodnight."

I was tired, but I couldn't fall asleep for what seemed hours. First I was thinking about Phil and about what my mother had said. Maybe she was right, but I didn't think so. Something would happen. The whole thing would probably blow over. And then I found myself thinking about Chuck's sister, Rachel.

I fell asleep thinking about her.

Chapter 6

The next Monday I saw Rachel four times: three times in the halls and once in study hall. I couldn't believe I'd never noticed her in study hall before. After that, I'd usually see her a couple of times a day. We'd smile to each other, but that was all. I thought about walking over to her and starting a conversation, but she was usually with one of her friends. Besides, knowing her opinion of football players, I was intimidated.

I wasn't doing any better with Phil than I was with Rachel. He seemed to be making it a point of honor to ignore me and hang out more and more with Greg. They spent a lot of time with Perry and his friends, driving around in Perry's car, or at least they spent a lot of time talking about it. Maybe Phil wanted me to think I was missing out on something groovy, but between football and a chemistry project that was due at the end of the week, I was glad to be left out. Chemistry is hardly my best subject. It seemed that every time I saw Phil, I was working on the project.

"You're becoming a regular horned-rimmed bookworm," he said one day, as he sat down next to me at lunch.

"Hardly," I said. "I'm just trying to make some sense out of this garbage."

"Need some help?" he asked with a touch of sarcasm.

I was desperate for help and Phil has a very scientific mind, but I would fail before I'd ask him for help. "No, thanks," I told him.

"Too bad. I thought that if I could help you, maybe you could come out with me and Perry after school. I noticed today's practice was called off. I thought maybe you'd just like to hang loose for an afternoon."

There was something in Phil's voice that made me think this was a serious offer, that he wasn't just suckering me into something. So I said, "Yeah, that sounds like fun." I missed Phil.

But it wasn't fun. The whole afternoon turned out to be a disaster. The only positive thing about it was that nobody except me realized what a total disaster it was. It began when I had to shove my way into the car with six other guys. There was something wrong with the exhaust so we had to keep the windows wide open and it was cold out. The stink from the exhaust made me sick to my stomach, even with the windows open, and then somebody started smoking. So I started, too. I knew I couldn't inhale, but I pretended I could and almost threw up all over everyone.

Luckily Perry had to get gas and I got out of the car and took as many deep breaths as I could before we started again. I managed to get a seat next to the window this time and spent the rest of the afternoon with my head hanging out.

The following Monday Phil asked me if I wanted to go racing around in Perry's car again.

"I'd like to, but I got practice today."

Phil looked at me like I was nuts and started to walk away. Then he stopped and when he turned around he was doing one of his Harold imitations.

"Hey, ah, gee, duh, Kenneee! What's the matter? You too good to be wid me and my brudder? Huh, Kenneee?" He began laughing like an ape and drooling.

"I gotta go," I said. "I'll be late."

He grabbed my arm and demanded, "What's the matter, Kenny? Am I losing my touch? You used to laugh. You too good to laugh now? You too good to spend the afternoon with Perry and his friends? I know a half-dozen guys who'd give anything to get an invitation like you just got."

I stared at him for a few seconds and I started to think about what my mother had said. "How come you always ask me to do things with you when I got football practice? I'll meet you around five. We can do something then," I suggested.

"No, man!" he shouted angrily. "You think Perry sets up his schedule by your cruddy football practice?"

"Okay, so we don't go with Perry. I didn't think it was so great anyway . . ."

"And you showed it. Let me tell you, you showed it. You too much of a goody-goody to smoke? What's the matter? You in training, so you don't smoke?"

"I don't even know how to smoke. If I'd tried once more I would have puked all over everyone . . ."

"You know what's the matter with you, Kenneee, baby? I'll tell you. You're getting so serious lately. Life's just one laugh—remember?"

Just then Perry's car pulled up to the curb and Perry began honking. "Let's go," he called out.

"Coming?" Phil dared me.

"I got practice. But I'll meet you at five . . ."

"Jock!" he jeered, and ran toward the car.

I hurried off to practice feeling strangely happy. At the last minute, despite the coach's temper, I'd almost changed my mind and gone with Phil.

Chapter 7

"Seven forty-five tomorrow morning—that's seven forty-five A.M., my friends," the coach said solemnly, and then grinned. "I want to see each and every one of you at the track. From now on, in rain, sleet or snow, we're going to run every morning for fifteen minutes. And I don't want to see any notes from your mothers telling me you can't do it because of the weather. If you want to play on this team, you be there."

If it hadn't been for the coach's inhuman approach to physical fitness, I probably never would have seen the yellow school bus coming down my street. Right away the bus caught my eye because I knew there were no kids on my block who rode one. It slowed down in front of the Harrigans' house and Harold came running out, practically pulling an old lady down the stairs with him. I thought it must be his grandmother, but it wasn't.

"Bye, Mommy! Bye!" Harold shouted.

He didn't have to shout because she was standing right next to him. She kissed him and he kissed her back about five times. They looked like wet, mushy kisses but she didn't seem to mind. When the bus door opened, Harold began shouting, "Morning, Scottie! Morning, Scottie!"

"How are you doing, my man?" the bus driver greeted him. "Got your maps today?"

"You bet, Scottie. I got them!" Harold shouted, waving some paper in the air. He hoisted his stiff body up the steps and the bus driver held out a hand to help. I got a good view of the driver then and I was surprised by what I saw. He was young, with longish hair and a fantastic Fu Manchu mustache.

"Good boy, Harold." The driver laughed good-naturedly. "Couldn't find my way to school without Harold and his maps." I could tell the driver liked Harold. I stayed and watched until the bus drove off.

All the way to school I thought about Harold and the old woman who was his mother instead of his grandmother. And about Scottie, the hip bus driver, and about Harold going off to school in a yellow school bus. He reminded me of a little kid. "Bye, Mommy! Bye!" Shouting. Waving. Kissing. Happy. Going off to school—except it wasn't a regular school. It had to be a retarded school, I thought, with a whole bunch of Harolds running around. And that was okay, too, because all the other retards probably grooved on Harold and he probably grooved on them. And best of all it meant he didn't just sit around all day and stare at nothing and collect rocks and wait for some smart-ass kid like Phil to come and make fun of him.

Every morning I'd watch Harold going off to school and every morning it was exactly the same scene. I liked watching it, too. There was something nice about the way Harold and his mother acted toward each other. I could tell she really liked his wet, slobby kisses.

She'd stand at the gate and wave to Harold until the bus turned the corner. And Harold would stick his goofy head out the window and wave back. If Harold's bus was late, Harold and his mother would be standing on the porch waiting when I'd pass by. If Harold saw me, which he usually did, he'd start screaming. "Hi, Kenny! Hi! Morning, Kenneee!"

I'd wave back and say, "Hi, Harold," and hurry on.

Then I could hear Harold say to his mother, or rather shout like he was telling the whole world, "That's Kenny, Mommy. He's my friend."

I was surprised that Harold remembered my name. I'd never spoken to him since that day with Phil.

In a strange way, I began to look forward to passing Harold and his mother in the morning. I went out of my way to be friendly. I thought maybe it would make up for the way Phil treated the kid.

When I got home from school one day, I saw my sister Patty and her friend Anita dancing on the front porch. Patty has one of those little portable phonographs and she was playing one of my records. I could hear it halfway down the street. That made me mad enough. I'd told that brat a hundred times to stay out of my room, not to mention my records, which I naturally kept in my room. But what I saw when I reached my house made me even madder.

Patty and Anita were dancing all right, but by the way their arms were flopping around and shooting out and their faces twisting into all crazy, ugly contortions,

I knew they were doing an imitation of a retard dancing. I just knew it.

I ran down the front walk and jumped up the steps, pushing Patty aside so hard she fell down. I grabbed my record and shouted at her, "The next time you touch one thing of mine, I'm going to cream you! *Understand?*"

At first, Patty was too terrified even to cry. I was home earlier than she'd expected. The coach had a meeting so practice was cut short.

"And another thing," I screamed. "I'd just like to know what you and Anita were dancing like?"

By this time Patty had begun to come out of shock. "None of your business," she told me.

"Yeah, well, I'm making it my business, Patty. I want to know if you and Anita were imitating that retarded kid who lives down the street?"

They began giggling.

"Were you?" I demanded.

"What if we were?" Patty laughed. Then she and Anita broke up again.

"Because it's not nice. See. It's mean!"

Patty laughed in my face. I hit her. She began screaming for my mother, who was already on her way out.

"What's going on here?" she demanded.

"Mommy! Kenny hit me!" Patty screamed. "He hit me for no reason. Didn't he, Anita?"

Anita nodded.

I wished I could have hit her, too.

"Kenny," my mother sighed.

"Don't go blaming me, Mom. Listen to my side for a change. Patty deserved to be hit and more."

"I did not. He's just mad because I took one of his dumb records."

My mother looked at Patty and then at me. "Patty," she sighed, "you've been told to leave Kenny's things alone. But, Kenny, that's no reason to hit her."

"That's not why I hit her, Mom," I groaned.

"All right, let's go inside and talk about it. The whole neighborhood doesn't have to hear our fights. I think you should go home, Anita."

"I think Anita should stay. She was part of it," I said.

We all went inside.

I told my mother about Anita and Patty dancing and imitating Harold. At first they denied it, but Patty's a lousy liar and my mother got the truth out of her. I have to hand it to my mother, she handled the whole thing pretty well. By the time she finished explaining to them why they shouldn't make fun of people like Harold, they felt like the two little twerps they are. I almost wished Phil could have heard her.

I didn't realize just how much he needed to hear Mom until the next Saturday. There wasn't a game, so I had the whole day to myself. I felt totally free. Not a care in the world. I slept late, fixed my own breakfast of half a pound of bacon and four eggs and English muffins. Then I went to lie down again because I was so stuffed I thought I was going to throw up. I was lying there, listening to some music, when Phil suddenly appeared.

"Hi, Kenny. How's things?" he said, smiling. He came over and sat down on the bed.

I was surprised and cautious. Phil had to have some other motive besides friendship.

"Fine, Phil. Things are okay. How about you?"

"Same old stuff, man. But no complaints. You know me. A laugh a minute." He picked up a *Sports Illustrated* that was lying on the bed and began thumbing through it without really looking at it. Then he said, "I've been thinking about you and me lately. All the good times we've had. It's a shame to let it all end like this."

I nodded noncommittally. I felt like I was being led into a trap and I wasn't in the mood to be zapped.

"Anyway, this whole thing with The Mental. It's just not the same. You and I could have had a ball with him. I mean, Herbie's a zero and Greg doesn't have your touch, Kenny."

"I don't know how to tell you this any better than I already have, but I'm just not interested in fooling around with some retarded kid."

"I know that, man. I got the message. But Harold likes you. He asks for you all the time. He tells me how he waves to you every morning. Now, that's sweet . . ."

"Cut it, Phil."

"Okay. Okay. You're right. I didn't come over here to have a fight, Kenny. I just thought since The Mental asks for you, and he knows you and I are friends—anyway, I'd just act like a go-between. I was just over at his house. He's outside. And believe me, Kenny, he asked for you. So I thought, since there's no game, I'd chance your being home."

I was still cautious. Phil was being too nice—or was I just being too suspicious? I decided to go with him.

"Wait till you see him and talk to him, Kenny," Phil said, as we left the house. "He's changed. Really changed. I know you think I've been screwing around with him, but I think you'll be impressed when you see how far he's come under my care!"

Harold was standing by the gate, looking down the street toward my house. As soon as he saw us, he started waving like crazy and calling our names.

Maybe I was wrong about Phil after all, I thought.

Harold threw his arms around me and practically kissed me when I stopped. "Kenny! Kenny! I like you, Kenny!"

"I like you, too, Harold," I gasped, unwrapping his arms from my neck.

"Be cool, Mental," Phil ordered. "I told you that mentals aren't supposed to fall all over people."

Harold frowned. "I sorry."

"That's okay, tomato brain. We all make mistakes. Even humans make mistakes." Phil laughed. He looked at me and demanded, "Funny?"

"It's a scream," I snapped.

"Hey, Mental, Kenny here thinks I'm being mean to you. Tell him. Am I ever mean to you?"

"No. Phil nice. Phil my friend. I like Phil."

"Okay, Harold, let's show Kenny how smart you are." Harold shook his head up and down. "Tell Kenny here—what's your name?"

Harold grinned proudly and began, "My name is Harold The Mental Havermeyer."

"Very good, Mental. And how do you spell that?"

"M-E-N-T-A-L."

"Where do you live?"

"I live here," he said, pointing eagerly to his house.

"The address! The address!" Phil demanded impatiently.

"1 2 3 Loony Bin Place."

"Gee, Kenneee, if The Mental here lives at 1 2 3 Loony Bin Place, you must live at 8 9 10 Loony Bin Place." Phil laughed long and hard at his joke. Then he said, "Hey, Kenny, The Mental here is doing a real good job and you haven't applauded him once. Not once. Now it's not nice to hurt a mental's feelings."

I wished I hadn't come, but I couldn't think of an easy way to leave without hurting Harold's feelings. I could tell he thought the sun rose and set with Phil.

"Now, Mental, I understand you go to school," Phil went on. "Can you tell your old pal, Kenny—and this is the one-hundred-thousand-dollar question—what is the address of your school?"

Harold grinned, stood up straight, and said, "ABC Retarded Row."

"Excellent. And what do you do in school?"

"We cook. We make things . . ."

"Not that, dummy. What did I tell you?"

"I pick my nose." Harold smiled. Then he frowned. "But my teacher said that not nice."

"Who's your best teacher. Harold?" Phil egged him on.

Harold smiled again. "You, Phil. You teach me."

"And what do you call your number-one teacher?"

"Master."

"Jesus Christ, Phil," I said, "this is sick. It's really sick!"

Phil didn't have time to answer because all of a sudden the front door flew open and some guy came charging down the front steps, waving his fist at us and shouting, "Get out of here, you crummy . . ."

Phil started running and I ran with him. But even as I ran, I could hear Harold. He shouts even louder when he's excited. "Don't be angry, Felix. They my friends."

Phil and I didn't stop running until we were five blocks away and ready to collapse.

"That was close," Phil gasped.

"Who was that?" I asked. I had a funny feeling Phil had set me up.

"How the hell do I know?"

"Are you sure?"

"Yeah, I'm sure. Do you think I would have run this far if I wasn't?"

"I don't know.'" I turned around to see if the guy was following us.

Phil nudged me and grinned. "So tell me, how do you like me as the master teacher of mentals?"

"You were great, Phil. I've never seen you so great," I said sarcastically.

"I get the distinct feeling you don't mean that."

"Yeah, well, let me ask you something."

"Be my guest."

"What are you doing this for? What's so interesting about a retard?"

"You got a point there. But then what's so interesting about anything? Running up and down a football field any better than The Mental?"

"A lot. This is really sick."

"Ah, yes, folks, let me introduce you to our All-American boy here, Kenneth P. Shea, protector of all that is good and wholesome, defender of that great American tradition of sportsmanship, not to mention the rights of retards. Is there anything I've forgotten?"

"Come on, Phil. Let's go some place and talk. You said something before, about all the good times . . ."

"Up yours, Kenny, baby. I wouldn't be caught dead talking to someone like you in front of anyone except a mental. You think you're so cool. You think you've got it made. But I'll tell you something, you're nothing. You don't even have your sense of humor anymore. Harold's better company than you. Better company and better conversation . . ."

"Sure, Phil, you finally made it, didn't you? Master of retards. Herbie, and Harold . . ."

Phil punched me. I was stunned but not hurt. I could have hit him back, but I didn't. He stood there for a few seconds, staring at me, waiting for me to swing.

I shrugged and started to leave.

"Mental Lover!" Phil screamed.

I kept on walking.

Chapter 8

How does something like this happen? I asked myself as I walked home. How do things get so far gone?
Was Phil flipping out? I didn't know. Maybe my
mother was right. Maybe he'd always been like this—
just not so obvious. The master bit. That was Phil. He
always wanted to be master. The mastermind of everything we did, of how and where we spent our time—
maybe even the master over me. And it was okay, as
long as I went along with it, but the minute I stopped
obeying him, the minute he thought he was losing
control . . .

No, it was too crazy to believe. Phil was my friend,
I thought, and friendships don't last forever. I've had
friends before whom I hardly speak to anymore. No
big deal. We've just grown apart. It's the same with
Phil. We've just grown apart.

When I reached my street, I looked around to see if
the guy who had chased us was anywhere around. He
was. He and Harold were in the front yard playing
ball. I stopped walking and considered turning around
and going the long way home so I wouldn't have to pass
by. But the long way home is about a five minute walk
and I wasn't in the mood for that; instead, I watched
them playing catch. Harold kept missing the ball, but
that didn't seem to bother him or the other guy. He

was laughing and talking to Harold a lot like the bus driver did.

I was so absorbed watching them that I didn't realize I had edged closer to get a better view until Harold called out, "There's Kenneee! Kenneee! Hi, Kenneee!"

The guy who had chased us looked at me. He didn't look too friendly and I thought of just waving to Harold and hurrying by. But I didn't. Instead, I began walking across the street and talking.

"Hiya, Harold," I said, trying not to sound too nervous. But my armpits were dripping like crazy, which is an awful feeling when it's about forty degrees out.

I looked at the guy who had chased us and said, "I'm really sorry about what happened."

"Listen, punk! Harold doesn't need your apologies. He doesn't need anything from scum like you. So get lost before I smear you all over the sidewalk."

I had no doubt from the size of this guy—he was at least six feet and must have weighed close to two hundred pounds—that he could do just what he said. But for some insane reason I didn't want to leave. Maybe I wanted to be smeared all over the sidewalk. I found myself apologizing again.

"I'm really sorry. I didn't like what was happening, either. I guess I should have said something. I know. That's why I'm sorry."

I don't know what changed his mind, but instead of smearing me all over the sidewalk the guy stared at me for a few seconds and said, "I'm Harold's brother, Felix Havermeyer. Feel like playing some catch?"

"Sure," I exclaimed.

So I stayed and we all played catch for a while. Then we wrestled. Let me tell you, it's quite an experience wrestling with Harold. It's kind of like wrestling with a liquefied robot.

"Come on back tomorrow if you want," Felix said when I left. "I'll be here around one."

"Thanks, maybe I will," I said. "So long. See you around, Harold."

Harold waved and called to me until I disappeared into my house.

I'm not sure why, but I went back to Harold's the next afternoon. It wasn't just because of Harold. I mean, I felt badly about what had happened with Phil, but I wasn't on any guilt trip. I wasn't getting any kicks out of being with Harold. Mainly it was because of Felix. I liked being with him. It was easy talking to him. He knew a lot about sports; and I know it's crazy, but he made playing catch with Harold fun.

Felix and Harold were sitting on the front steps talking and laughing when I got there. I wondered what they could be talking about. The thought of carrying on a normal conversation with Harold seemed impossible.

When Harold saw me, he gave me one of his sloppy, happy grins and came hobbling down the stairs, his arms outstretched like he was going to hug me.

Felix came to my rescue. "Take it easy, Harold." He laughed. "I told you that you don't have to hug everyone who comes to visit. See, this is what adults do. They shake hands and say, 'Hello, Kenny. I'm glad you could come.' "

48

"Okay, Felix, I'm sorry," Harold eagerly apologized. He stood back from me and repeated exactly what Felix had said, and then we shook hands.

We played some more ball. It was like teaching a five-year-old except harder. A five-year-old is more coordinated than Harold. We threw the ball over and over and he kept missing, which is pretty hard considering we were playing with a basketball! But Felix never lost his patience. He never got bored repeating the same thing over and over again. He never made Harold look stupid.

Then wonders of all wonders, Harold began catching more and more balls. When he caught two in a row, you'd have thought he'd just hit a home run out of Yankee Stadium.

"I did it! I did it!" he shouted, jumping up and down on one foot.

"Okay, that was good. Let's see if you can do it again," Felix said.

"Okay, Felix. Throw!"

We threw some more and, after ten minutes, Harold set a record—six catches in a row. Felix and I went wild congratulating him and telling him how fantastic he was. Harold loved it. So did Felix.

"Now there's one great kid," he said to me with pride. "Thirteen years vegetating in an institution and look at him. I'll make a ballplayer out of him yet!" He laughed.

"I'm thirsty," Harold announced. "Did you bring soda, Felix?"

"You'd better believe it. Didn't I promise?"

"Yes!" Harold shouted, and began hobbling toward the house.

"Oh, Jesus, what a sight," Felix moaned, and we went inside.

"I'm so very happy to see you, Kenny." Mrs. Havermeyer smiled when Felix introduced us. "I've never had the pleasure of actually meeting Kenny, but I see him in the morning. Right, Harold?" She turned back to me and went on. "You're on your way to school when Harold gets on his bus."

I nodded. "I just live down the street," I said.

"Yes, I know," Mrs. Havermeyer said, and smiled again. She was smiling a lot but I had the distinct feeling she was sizing me up—like she didn't trust me. I guess I couldn't blame her.

We all went into the kitchen. There was a big bowl of homemade cookies on the kitchen table. Immediately Harold's hand shot for the bowl.

"No, Harold. Guests first," Mrs. Havermeyer said patiently.

Harold pouted and she squeezed his hand gently.

"Get a plate for your friend, Harold. Here, Kenny, take as many as you like."

Before I had a chance to take one, Harold's hand flashed in front of me to the cookies.

"You were told to wait!" Felix shouted. "Don't be greedy."

"Don't yell at him," Mrs. Havermeyer said. "You'll only confuse him." And then she said to Harold, "Sit down and you can have all the cookies you want."

No sooner did she say that than he sat down and

50

grabbed a handful of cookies, stuffing one in his mouth.

"You're a slob!" Felix shouted disgustedly.

"Leave him alone," Mrs. Havermeyer snapped.

"But, Mom," Felix pleaded. "He's never going to learn . . ."

"He'll learn. He'll learn, but not if you're always on top of him for every little thing. Take it easy with him. He's only home a month." Then she said to Harold. "You like Mommy's cookies, don't you?"

Harold's answer was a grin and a dribble of cookie crumbs down his chin.

Felix sighed and poured the soda. "Where's Pop?" he asked.

"Sleeping," Mrs. Havermeyer said. "He always falls asleep when he's reading the paper." Then she turned to me and said, "Felix tells me you're a nice boy—not like the others. And you know, Felix, it's funny, but I've noticed Kenny. I have. The way he looks at Harold. It's different from the others. And when you told me the terrible things those boys taught Harold, I thought, that boy I see in the morning can't be teaching Harold those things. And then I thought, he looks like such a nice boy. I wish he could be Harold's friend. I know it's silly. But then I'd say to myself, 'Why would a normal, healthy boy want to be friends with my Harold?' "

"Come on, Mom," Felix sighed.

Mrs. Havermeyer blew her nose. "Leave me alone, Felix. I'm entitled. After all these years, I'm entitled to some little happy foolish thoughts about Harold. You don't mind, do you, Kenny?"

"No," I said, and I really didn't mind. But I knew how Felix felt. I guess I'd feel the same if my mother began acting gushy over someone I'd brought home. I looked at Harold to see what he thought of all this. He was busy eating; he couldn't have cared less.

"Kenny, do you have a bat and mitt?" Felix said suddenly.

"Sure."

"What do you think about teaching old Harold here how to bat?"

"Why not?" I said. I'd done stupider things in my life than teach a retard how to bat . . .

"What do you say, Harold?" Felix asked, pulling the plate of cookies out of his reach.

"I want more!" Harold cried.

"Look at me," Felix demanded. "If you want to sit around and stuff food into your face all day, go ahead. But I'm not staying for that . . ."

"Felix!" Mrs. Havermeyer cried.

"Please, Mom. I'm not going to spend my time babying him. You do enough of that all week. That's not why I come and that's not what Kenny's here to watch. That's not why we brought Harold home. If you want him to get better, then you've got to stop feeling sorry for him. He's eighteen, not five. You gotta stop treating him like that."

I don't think Harold understood what Felix was saying. He looked mostly confused. Sad when he looked at his mother and frightened when he looked at his brother.

"Kenny, would you mind getting the bat and ball?" Felix asked.

"Sure, sure thing," I said. I wanted to get out of that house. I can't stand my own family fights, much less somebody else's.

"You will come back, won't you?" Mrs. Havermeyer asked. Except she wasn't asking. It was more like pleading.

"Mom, please." Felix's patience was wearing thin. "Come on, Kenny. I'll see you out."

We were on the front porch and Felix began, "I'm really sorry about what happened inside. I should have expected it. It's hard for my mother. She loves that goofy kid so much."

"Hey, it's okay. I understand," I insisted.

"You don't have to come back if you don't want to. I mean, you don't have to feel obligated to us."

"I know. I want to come back. I just can't wait to see if Harold can hit a ball!"

"You mean that, don't you?"

"Sure I mean it. Why else would I say it?" Which wasn't exactly true. I could have gotten along fine without ever seeing Harold hit a ball.

"You're okay, Kenny," Felix said warmly, and shook my hand.

That's when I was glad I'd said what I'd said.

When I came back with the ball and mitt, Felix said, "I was thinking, I have a friend who has two season tickets to the Giants. Want to go sometime?"

"Are you kidding? I'd give anything to see the Giants play!"

"Ever been to a game?"

"No. My father isn't too big on football."

"Okay, I'll talk to my friend this week. He'll be

away for the next home game. Maybe I can get those tickets."

"I can pay for the ticket," I said.

"Forget it, Kenny. My treat. I don't know anyone else who likes football, either. My wife can't stand it."

That surprised me. I didn't think Felix was old enough to be married.

Then he added, "Anyway, it's more fun going to the game with another football nut."

"That's what I am!"

"You're more than that, Kenny. You're a nice kid. I'm sorry I came on so strong yesterday."

"Forget it. How did you know? I don't blame you. I guess I would have been pretty upset, too, if Harold was my brother and someone was doing what Phil was doing. Do you think Harold understood?"

"Nah, he likes the creep. He'll probably even miss him for a while. What's his name?"

"Phil."

"Yeah, Phil. The kid's got problems."

I nodded but didn't say anything. I think Felix understood that I didn't want to talk about Phil.

"So what else do you do besides football and spend your weekends helping out a retarded boy?" Felix asked.

"Not much."

"Go out?"

"With girls?"

Felix laughed. "That's the general idea."

I laughed too and shook my head.

"Don't have the time?" he asked.

"I guess I'd find the time if I could find the girl," I admitted. And then I began telling him about Rachel Simon. I hadn't told anyone about her, but Felix was just the kind of a guy you tell.

"That reminds me of a thing I had for a girl when I was in high school," he said. "Her name was Carrie Bethune and I thought she was fantastic."

"Did you go out with her?"

He laughed. "I finally got up the nerve to ask her out."

"And?"

"And not much. We went out, but it was a total flop. You're not going to believe this, Kenny, but I couldn't think of a thing to say to her. Luckily we were going to the movies so that killed most of the night, but afterward—I don't think I said two words to her! She must have thought I was the biggest jerk she'd ever met."

"I don't think that would happen to Rachel and me. I've never met a girl I could talk to so easily."

"So why don't you ask her out?"

"I wish I knew. I guess it's basically because I'm afraid she'll say no."

"What girl would say no to a good-looking football player!" He laughed.

"That's the problem—I'm on the football team. So is her brother. She thinks we're all a bunch of jerks!"

"That's a new one."

"Typical of my luck," I sighed.

Chapter 9

There was a note on my desk in English class on Monday morning. It was edged in black and it said, "How's The Mental? Did he teach you how to pick your nose?"

I crumpled it up.

Phil was waiting for me in the hall after class.

"Hey, Kenneee, baby! Feeling okay?"

I was going to ignore him totally but then I decided that was exactly what he wanted, so I said, "I feel great."

"No signs yet?"

"I'm not interested, Phil . . ."

"But I'm worried about you," he taunted. "I thought you might be showing signs of the mental fever."

"You aren't doing a thing to me, so save it," I said as calmly as I could.

"Sorry, Kenny, I can't help it. You're just so funny. Playing catch with a retard and some muscle man who threatened to tear us apart."

It was pointless to talk to him. I started to leave.

Phil began walking next to me. "Yeah, I saw you playing catch with The Mental. And I was touched. Really touched. Right here." He belched.

"That guy who chased us happens to be Harold's brother."

"Well, ain't that sweet now. It's nice to know The Mental has someone looking after his interests."

"With people like you, he needs it."

"Touché, Kenny. Touché." He laughed. "That was clever—for a Mental Lover. And it hurt. It cut me to the quick."

"Shove it," I told him.

Phil grabbed hold of my arm and called to Greg, who was coming out of the science room. "Hey, Greg, look who showed up."

"I don't believe it!" Greg gasped.

"Yup, it's our old friend, Kenneee."

"And here we thought he was dying of the mental fever!"

"But we gotta watch him carefully. He's showing advanced signs," Phil went on.

"That bad?"

"I'm afraid so. He's acting very sensitive this morning. His feelings got hurt. And do you believe it—he told his best friend to shove it."

Greg was giggling like the fool he is and I'd had it. "Drop dead, Hillman," I said angrily, and pushed by him.

"Wait up, Kenneee!" He laughed and tried to put his arm around me. "I'll help you to your next class."

I jabbed him in the gut with my elbow.

He moaned.

Phil laughed.

I headed to my next class.

All week Phil and Greg kept up the mental thing. It bothered me, but I tried not to let it show any more than I already had. I knew that was all Phil needed.

He wanted to push me till I blew my cool. I decided I wasn't going to. I acted like he didn't exist. I guess that got to him more than anything else I could have done because on Thursday the inevitable happened.

It came in a roundabout way, so I wasn't prepared for it. I was sitting at a lunch table with Chuck. We were the only ones there and Chuck had dumped his books on one of the empty chairs.

Phil and Greg came over. "Mind moving your books," Phil said to me. I guess he thought Chuck's books were mine.

"I mind," Chuck snapped back. "They're mine and the seat's taken. In fact, the whole table is taken."

"By who? Your books and The Mental Lover?"

"You got it, funny man," Chuck answered.

"Move them, Simon. I'm sitting here," Phil insisted. I began to wonder if Phil had lost his sanity. Chuck is twice his size and could flatten him without any problems.

"Like I said, the seat's taken," Chuck repeated.

"Hey, Mental Lover, move the books," Phil ordered me.

Before I could say anything, Chuck answered, "You're not wanted here."

Phil ignored Chuck and said to me, "Come on, Mental Lover, and do an old friend a favor."

I saw Chuck's fist tighten. I didn't want him fighting my battles and besides, Phil wasn't bothering me. I thought Phil was acting pretty dumb, so I said, "I don't care if he sits here."

"Well, I do," Chuck said. "I don't want any skinny,

two-bit comedian sitting here boring me with this mental-fever crap. Who is this creep anyway?" he said to me. And without waiting for an answer he said to Phil, "I've had enough from you. If you got something against retarded people keep it to yourself."

I felt that something totally above my head was going on between Phil and Chuck. I couldn't understand why he was so angry at Phil and I didn't think it had anything to do with me. But I didn't have time to ask any more questions.

"Butt out, Simon!" Phil ordered, and knocked Chuck's books off the seat.

Chuck was up in an instant and he lunged for Phil.

I stood up—just in time to catch Chuck's fist in my shoulder. I'd never felt pain like that before. Chuck must have a fist of steel.

Phil began laughing. That was all I needed. I went for him, punching like crazy, and he began punching back. I could hear kids calling my name. Some kids were cheering for Phil. And we kept punching each other, rolling all over the floor, knocking over chairs.

I heard a voice boom: "Break it up! Break it up!" It was Mr. Fry, the lunchroom teacher. Usually he sits in a corner, eating his sandwiches and drinking his coffee and reading his newspaper. He's so quiet and innocuous nobody notices him. He never interferes unless a fight breaks out, but when it does, he's there, all two hundred pounds. I knew I should listen to him, but Phil wasn't letting up. I wasn't about to let him get in the last punch.

"I said to break it up, you numskulls!" Mr. Fry

bellowed. As he spoke, I felt one of his enormous hands grasp my shoulder and pull Phil and me apart with such force that I landed flat on my back, underneath a lunch table.

"Get up, you miserable creeps!" Mr. Fry shouted.

My lip was bleeding and my shoulder ached. I looked at Phil. Blood was gushing from his nose.

"Detention hall all next week for the two of you," Mr. Fry said flatly. That was Mr. Fry—judge, jury, and executioner of the cafeteria. When he pronounced sentence, there was no appeal. To speak could mean detention hall for life.

"Wipe your nose, Canady," Mr. Fry ordered.

"It won't stop bleeding," Phil complained.

"You and Shea clean up this mess and then go to the nurse's office." Mr. Fry went back to his coffee and paper like nothing had happened.

Phil and I cleaned up. Phil's nose still hadn't stopped bleeding, so he went to the nurse. Greg tagged along beside him. I let them go.

"Look, Kenny, I'm sorry about that punch," Chuck said, as he helped me pick up the books. "That creep went too far. I know he's your friend, but . . ."

"Was—past tense."

"Well, somebody had to shut him up. He was getting to me with his jokes about that retarded kid. I'm sorry about detention hall, too. I mean, I started the fight."

"It was my fight. Mine and Phil's. It's been awhile in coming," I said, trying to laugh. My lip hurt. "The lunchroom is just about the worst place to have it.

What do you think the coach will say—about the detention?"

"First he'll probably kill you and after that he'll probably talk to Fry and work something out."

I groaned. "Thanks. I needed that."

Chapter 10

The first time I saw Rachel the next morning, she waved to me and came over. "Hi. Remember me?"

"Sure. Hi, Rachel."

"Want to have lunch together today?"

"Sure," I gulped, and my voice cracked.

"You do have fifth period lunch?"

"Every day."

"I thought so." She smiled. "See you then. I'll meet you outside the cafeteria."

My next class was French but it might as well have been Chinese for all I got out of it. All I could think about was Rachel and what had made her want to have lunch with me today.

She was waiting for me when I got to the cafeteria. "There's a small table next to Mr. Fry. Mind if we sit there?"

"Ah, Mr. Fry. My favorite person,'" I sighed.

"I know. But what did you expect—having a fight like that in the lunchroom?"

"I didn't plan the fight."

"I know." She laughed. "I'm not blaming you. I just asked you what you expected Mr. Fry to do?"

"Throw me halfway across the lunchroom floor?"

"That'll teach you, anyway." She laughed again.

"You're all heart."

"I've been told that before!"

We made our way through the lunchroom to the table next to Fry. It was vacant, of course. Nobody in his or her right mind sits there; but I was getting the distinct feeling that Rachel was a screwball.

We sat down and she took out her sandwich and unwrapped it. "Oh, crap," she mumbled. "Egg salad. I hate egg salad."

I opened mine. "I have tuna. Want to trade?"

"You like egg salad?"

"Not as much as tuna."

"That wasn't my question. I asked if you liked egg salad."

"I can get it down in an emergency."

"Good!" she exclaimed, reaching for my sandwich, "because this is what I call an emergency." She took a bite out of my sandwich and sighed, "Hmm, good. I'm glad I asked you to have lunch with me today."

"So am I. As a matter of fact, I was thinking to myself just before I met you, if only once in my life my mother would pack an egg-salad sandwich for me. And here it is—you're like an answer to my most secret, heartfelt wish, Rachel."

"You're so sweet, Kenny. And a martyr, too. That shows strength of character." She laughed, starting on the other half of my sandwich. Then she added, "Go on and eat. That egg-salad sandwich may disintegrate if it's not eaten soon."

I looked at the sandwich. She was right. It was soggy and falling apart. I picked it up and half the egg salad fell out.

"No backsies!" Rachel laughed. She took another

bite of my sandwich and handed it back to me. "Here, you can have what's left. I'm not mad about tuna, either!"

"You're a nut!"

"Really, I feel badly about this trade. Why don't we get some ice cream for dessert?"

I held up the egg-salad sandwich and cried, "Dessert! What's the main course?"

"You wait here and I'll get the ice cream. What kind do you like? Sandwich or pop?"

"Sandwich."

She started off and was back in a minute. "Oh, I forgot, I don't have any money."

"Oh, no!" I moaned, reaching into my pocket. "Chuck was right about you."

"Well, it all works out because I did buy you a soda at Nino's that night."

"Come on, I'll walk you to the ice-cream machine. You may make off with my fifty cents."

"Oh, I bet Chuck told you I'm a thief, too."

"As a matter of fact, he has mentioned it once or twice."

"What other deep dark family secrets did he tell you?"

"Besides the fact that your mother is spending time for grand larceny?"

"He didn't?"

"He did."

"I can trust you not to let it go any further? I mean, it could ruin my reputation if such a thing got around school."

"Ah ha! And what kind of reputation do you have?"

"The worst! The absolute worst!"

"I think I'm beginning to like you, Rachel."

"Men, they're all alike," she sighed, dropping the quarter into the machine.

After we got the ice cream, we went back to the little table next to Mr. Fry. I felt like I was in a dream. Rachel was like no other girl I'd ever met. When we sat down, she stared at me for a few seconds and then said, "You know why I asked you to have lunch with me today?"

"No, but I have to admit, I've been wondering."

"It's because I think you're a really nice guy. I mean really nice. Nice-nice."

I know I was blushing. This was too good to be true. "Is this the part where the guy says, 'Shucks, honey, I bet you say that to all the guys'?"

She smiled and began playing with the ice-cream wrapper, tearing it into shreds. "No, I mean it. I saw you the other day playing with the retarded boy."

"Wow, it seems like the whole world drove by that day. I didn't notice anyone."

"Chuck was driving me over to Susan Bellamy's house. We're working on a history project together."

"I know Susan. She lives a few blocks away. But how did you know the kid was retarded?"

"I know retarded people. I can tell when I see one. And besides, with all that crap your friend Phil . . ."

"Ex-friend."

"So I gather." She smiled self-consciously for the first time. "Anyway, I was getting pretty sick of his imitations and mental jokes. Boy, he really had it coming to him. I wish I could have socked him one."

"How come you know retards?" I asked.

"We had a retarded sister," she told me.

I looked at her for a second, speechless.

"Don't worry. I'm not uptight about it, Kenny. Laurie was my sister. She happened to be retarded. But I loved her. She was the greatest kid I ever knew."

"So that's why Chuck got so mad at Phil yesterday." She nodded.

"I'm sorry I acted so surprised," I apologized. "I guess I was though. I didn't know."

"That's okay. Why should you know? Anyone who knows us knows about Laurie. We never hid it or anything."

Rachel had a point. She and Chuck live on the other side of town and Baldwin is a pretty big town as towns go. There are four elementary schools, two different junior highs and then we all merge for high school.

Rachel went on. "Laurie was probably the most important thing that's happened to me, to my whole family. Someone like Laurie brings you all together, Kenny. It's like you want to give her all the love and good times you can," she sighed. "So anyway, I knew the kid I saw you with was retarded and I knew what was going on with Phil the Crud and after yesterday, well anyway, I just wanted to tell you that I think you're nice."

I felt my head swelling—first Felix and now Rachel. I said, "Harold, the retarded kid—he's really okay. I got a kick playing with him and his brother."

"The other guy? The big guy with the mustache?"

"Yeah, his name's Felix. He's a really cool guy."
And then I came up with what I thought was a brainstorm. "Hey, Rachel, I'd really like to meet your sister someday."

Rachel got this odd, flushed look and then she looked at me and said, "Laurie's dead. She died two years ago."

"Hey, I'm sorry."

"Don't sweat it, Kenny. Really. It doesn't bother me anymore. In some ways it was even better. She had so many things wrong with her besides just being retarded. Mostly she had problems with her lungs. That's why she died. It was two weeks before her sixth birthday."

"Wow," I sighed.

"Nobody even expected her to live that long."

"Did she live at home?" I asked, remembering what Felix had told me about Harold.

"She was in and out of the hospital. It was so hard on Mom and Dad. Their whole lives revolved around Laurie, especially Mom's. But they're super, Kenny. I mean, when I think about it now, all they were going through with Laurie—but Chuck and I never thought it should be any other way. I mean, we never resented Laurie or anything like that. When Laurie died I felt like I wanted to die, too." She paused and then said, "You know something, Kenny? All those things wrong with Laurie and she was always laughing. Nothing bothered her except all the needles. She hated going to the doctor."

We didn't say anything for a few minutes. We sat there, eating our melting ice cream. I looked at Rachel every now and then. She seemed so far away, as if she was thinking about her sister. It may sound strange, but I felt special being with Rachel then. Here I was, almost a perfect stranger and I knew that she had just shared something very personal. I wanted to get to know Rachel better.

"Would you like to meet Harold?" I asked.

"Sure!"

"I told his brother I'd come over Sunday afternoon. That's when Felix is there. He's a great guy. You'll like him."

The bell rang for the next period and I went to math. Rachel had gym. I didn't learn much the rest of the day either. I kept on thinking about Rachel, going over every minute we'd spent together and everything we'd said to each other and everything I'd felt. The whole thing was weird. Weird and wonderful. But mostly I kept on thinking about her smile and the way she laughed. I loved the way she laughed.

As soon as I got home I played with the idea of calling her. I knew I had to—to make our plans more definite. We hadn't decided on a time to meet. But whenever I picked up the phone to call, I began feeling nauseous. I decided to wait until after dinner.

I was helping my mother with the dishes when the phone rang. Patty answered it. She came barging into the kitchen. "It's for you, Kenny! And it's a *girl!*"

"Shut up!" I shouted, and threw the towel in her face.

"Hi, Kenny. This is Rachel," came the voice from the other end of the phone. "I just wanted to check up about Sunday. You know, the time and stuff."

"I was going to call you!"

"Well, I'm going out now and I'm staying at a friend's house so I thought I'd get it all set up. Chuck said he'd drive me over about two. Okay?"

"Great. Want to meet me at my house or Harold's?"

"I can just go to his house—if you can tell his brother I'm coming."

"Yeah, sure. Felix comes over every Saturday, too. I'll stop by tomorrow and tell him."

"That's great, Kenny. I don't want to be barging in or anything."

"You won't. Wait till you meet Harold's mother. She'll probably go ape over you."

"Okay, Kenny, I gotta go. See you around two."

"See you."

It took me a long time to fall asleep that night. I couldn't get Rachel out of my mind. I couldn't help wondering who she was going out with tonight.

Chapter 11

It was like old home week when Rachel met the Havermeyers. She's anything but shy and withdrawn. She treated Harold like a long-lost friend and he was all over her in two seconds. When she told Mrs. Havermeyer that she'd had a retarded sister who'd died, Mrs. Havermeyer practically cried. "I have to get my husband! He has to meet you, Rachel," she exclaimed, returning almost instantly with Mr. Havermeyer.

I hadn't seen him before. He looked much older than Mrs. Havermeyer, tired and like he wasn't too healthy. He smiled at Rachel and me and then said to Harold in a soft, gentle voice, "You see what a popular boy you are, Harold. Not only one but two friends. You should be very happy."

"I am, Daddy," Harold promised.

"And be good and listen to your brother and your new friends. Don't make a nuisance out of yourself."

"I won't, Daddy."

Then Mr. Havermeyer disappeared again. Mrs. Havermeyer ushered us all into the kitchen for some of her famous cookies and Rachel and Felix and she talked on and on about Harold and Rachel's sister and retardates. Harold stuffed his mouth. I sat there feeling as left out as Harold. Finally there was a lull in the conversation and I glanced at Rachel. She gave me a look that meant "Help!" and I knew she wanted to get away from Mrs. Havermeyer as much as I did.

Then Harold grabbed the last cookie and Felix tried to get it out of his iron fist. I looked at Mrs. Havermeyer and smiled nervously and tried to think of a way out. It was Rachel who came up with the escape route. "Anyone for a walk!" she exclaimed.

"Great!" I said.

"Sounds good to me," Felix added. "Come on, Harold! We're going for a walk."

"Want to come, Mrs. Havermeyer?" Rachel asked, like she really meant it.

I breathed a sigh of relief when Mrs. Havermeyer said, "No, you kids go on together. It's enough to see Harold walking down the street with you." Her eyes looked like she was going to cry.

Felix put his arm around his mother and hugged her. Then he turned to Harold and said, "Get your things."

"I like walks!" Harold announced. "You like walks, Rachel?"

"Yeah, Rachel loves walks." Felix laughed and pushed Harold into the hall.

Mrs. Havermeyer followed right behind and began dressing Harold. She helped him on with his jacket and buttoned the buttons. Felix was getting annoyed again, and when Mrs. Havermeyer began putting on Harold's hat, he blew his stack. "Mom, he's gotta do it himself."

"Leave me alone," she said, and finished dressing him.

"Bye, Mommy, I'm going for a walk!" Harold shouted.

Rachel immediately grabbed Harold's hand and pulled him out the door and down the front steps. Harold looked pretty funny hobbling beside her and I couldn't help laughing.

Felix laughed, too. "I've never seen him go so fast!"

It was a nice day for a walk and the thought occurred to me that it would have been nicer if Harold and Felix weren't along. The sun was shining and there was even a slight white crusty remainder of an early snow that had fallen the night before. Good football weather. Harold and Rachel ran ahead, jumping in the snow and laughing. They were quite a sight.

"Do much skating?" Felix asked.

"Some. I fool around at hockey. Nothing serious."

"I used to play . . ." he began, when Rachel joined us.

"Play what?" she asked.

"Hockey," said Felix. "Like skating?"

"Love it," she said, and then she stared at Felix and said, "God, it must have been so awful for Harold in the institution."

"It was," Felix answered.

"In a way, I guess maybe it was better that Laurie died," Rachel said to Felix. "I mean, the time might have come when we'd have had to put her in an institution."

"Maybe not," Felix answered. "There are other alternatives, like the school that Harold's in. There's a lot of people who think the institutions should be shut down altogether and only have day schools and half-way houses were retarded people live together and take care of themselves. Something like dorms, with house parents. There are other alternatives now."

"Are all the institutions so bad?" Rachel asked.

"I don't know. I only know about the one Harold was in. It was dark and depressing. He wasn't mal-treated, but he wasn't well treated. He simply wasn't cared for," Felix said angrily. "It was just a whole bunch of retarded people living together with nothing to do all day. Just about nothing. You know, sit around and watch TV or look at magazines they can't read. There was one girl who spent her whole life look-ing at the telephone book. All day, all she did was sit and methodically turn the pages."

"Wasn't there anyone to help them or teach them?" Rachel asked.

"Not many. It was badly understaffed and most of the people had little training. They were happy so long as nobody acted up too much. And then every Saturday night there was a dance. I guess that was the best thing they had."

"Didn't they teach them *anything?*" Rachel re-peated.

"Not much. You saw the way he eats. Stuffing his mouth. And let me tell you, that was good today. You should have seen him when he first got home. He just shoveled the food in as fast as he could. Half the time he ate with his hands. Half the food landed on the floor. It was disgusting."

"He's not that bad now," I said.

"No, he's coming along pretty well. That's what keeps me going. It was the institution. We never should have sent him there. He wasn't that bad when he went in."

It was on the tip of my tongue to ask Felix why they had put Harold in the institution in the first place, but I figured that was a personal question and Felix would tell us if he wanted to. Rachel obviously felt differently because she asked, "How come you sent him there, then? How come you didn't just put him in the school he's in now?"

I thought Rachel was being nosy, but Felix only shrugged sadly and said, "My parents had no choice. There weren't any schools like that when Harold was little. At least not anywhere near where we lived. A local Catholic church had a school set up in its basement. It wasn't much, but it was better than nothing. At least it got him out of the house for a few hours every day. You can imagine how hard it was on my mother—never able to go anywhere. It wasn't like she could just ask a neighbor to watch him. I mean, she could have. He was a perfectly okay kid. Not at all violent. He just played by himself."

"Yeah, that's the way Laurie was, too. But she was in and out of the hospital so much it was just kinda nice when she was home," Rachel said.

"Anyway, there was this school," Felix went on. "One teacher for ten retarded kids between the ages of five and ten and one or two parent volunteers. One day when they were playing outside, Harold wandered off. Nobody could find him for hours. The police finally found him—tied to a tree in the park."

"What!" Rachel cried.

I felt a little sick to my stomach.

"I'm serious. Some kids or some sicky must have tied him to a tree as a joke. Sick, eh? God knows what else they did to him."

"Did you ever find out who did it?" I asked.

"No. But Harold really freaked out afterward. When they found him he was absolutely silent and wouldn't respond to anyone for days. That's when he started walking funny and tightening up his body. And all of a sudden he'd freak out. In the morning, in the middle of the day, or sometimes he'd wake up screaming. He'd scream and yell and bite himself. The teacher couldn't handle it. Not that we blamed her. So he left the program and he got worse and worse after that.

"My mother couldn't take having him home all day. That's when she made the decision. It was hard. I remember my father didn't want to put him in the institution, but he knew what it was doing to my mother. I was about twelve then and I couldn't believe they were sending Harold away.

"And then he had a hard time adjusting, too. We went to see him a lot. My parents went almost every weekend for thirteen years. He came home at Christmas and Thanksgiving. But it was hard . . ."

Felix's voice cracked at this point and he stopped talking.

"Oh, my God," Rachel cried, and turned to me. The tears were streaming down her face. "I can see someone like Phil tying a retarded kid to a tree."

I shrugged and half-whispered, "The same idea crossed my mind."

Chapter 12

Thanksgiving came and went and so did the football season. Baldwin didn't come in first, but we had a good year anyway; and the coach was as pleased as he could be considering we didn't win the league title.

It was a kind of relief when the season was over. I was exhausted and my first quarter grades showed it. My father wasn't pleased, so I promised the next quarter I'd do better.

I did try to study harder, but there was one major obstacle: Rachel. I think I was falling in love with her. I couldn't stop thinking about her. Every time I tried to read, I'd end up thinking about her, about something she said or something we'd done together. Instead of dreaming about running out football patterns, I was daydreaming about Rachel—but daydreams about Rachel were better because Rachel was better, even better than football. There was one problem. I was the only person who knew how I felt.

Except maybe Phil—not that I ever talked to him about Rachel. I hadn't talked to him at all since the lunchroom fight, so I figured the only way he could have suspected anything about Rachel and me was by following us on Sunday when we went to the Havermeyers'.

One day when I left study hall to go to the bathroom, I saw Phil leaning against the wall, with his arms folded and his body slouched. He was the only person in the hall. As soon as he saw me, he straightened up and grinned, as if he had been waiting for me. He said, "Cool, Kenny. Real cool—you and The Mental chick. I like it. It fits."

Then he turned and left before I could respond. But it didn't matter. I was so shocked I couldn't have thought of anything to say anyway.

Another time Phil and Greg were waiting for me after a class. Without saying anything they fell in beside me, one on each side, and Phil began, in a German accent, "I hear the subject Shea is having a romantic entanglement with another suspected Mental Lover subject."

"True, true, mein Kampf," Greg said. "Our records show the disease is spreading."

"It must be erradicated immediately!" Phil exclaimed. And then they took off, laughing.

Phil did other things, too, like appearing out of nowhere and doing an imitation of Harold. Or he'd pass me in the hall and make some dumb remark. Or I'd find an unsigned note in my desk about The Mental or mental fever. A couple of times I even got phone calls that were just heavy breathing. I knew it was Phil, but I never said anything about it to him. In fact, I never took him up on anything he did, because I knew that's what he wanted me to do. I hadn't been his friend for all those years without knowing his personal style of Chinese water torture. Besides, I thought it was pretty infantile stuff and it didn't bother me much. The only thing that bugged me was the thought of his keeping tabs on me. I figured if I ever saw him following Rachel and me, I'd do something. But I never saw him. If he was following us, he kept out of sight.

Phil may have picked up on the way I felt about Rachel, but one thing for sure—Rachel hadn't. I had the feeling that she thought of me more as an extension of her relationship with Felix and Harold than as me, a person, or, in particular, as me, a boy. Outside of school, I only saw her on Sunday afternoons at the Havermeyers'. The afternoons were her idea. She wanted to spend time with Harold. She thought she could help him.

At first I was bored by the whole thing with Harold and I only went because of Rachel. I knew she'd go even if I didn't. Sometimes she went on Saturdays and she and Felix did things with Harold, the same kinds of things we all did on Sundays, like exercising, teaching him how to eat, and talking with him. If Harold did well, Felix would take us all out to the coffee shop for something to eat. Harold loved to eat out.

Gradually I began to like these afternoons. They were fun in a way. We laughed a lot. Felix and Rachel were really into improving Harold. The two of them were crazy about him and because they loved him so much, they could tease him without hurting his feelings. We all laughed at Harold and with him; but it was different from the way it had been with Phil. I think part of spending time with Harold was learning to laugh at his craziness and learning to love him. I'm not sure I really did—not the way Felix and Rachel did.

One week I missed going on Sunday. My whole family had to visit my grandparents. When I saw Harold the next week, I was amazed at how much he seemed to have improved. I couldn't put my finger on exactly why, but he didn't seem so retarded anymore. He wasn't walking like a robot. He wasn't shouting so much.

Rachel decided we should all celebrate with a Walt Disney movie. Felix drove us to the theater and picked us up. "Do you mind if I don't go with you? I can't stand these movies," he said.

"That's fine," Rachel said.

"You're sure? I don't think Harold will be a problem."

"I'm telling you, it'll be fine," Rachel insisted. "Right, Harold?"

Harold grinned. "I like movies!"

After that we tried to do things on the weekends besides just hanging out at the Havermeyers'. One week we went sleigh riding and another we went to a museum. The only time Felix didn't come with us was when we went to the movies.

One day at lunch Rachel came over to me and said, "I have to talk to you, Kenny. The table near Mr. Fry is empty."

"Sure." We hadn't eaten together since that first time.

"I have the most terrible story to tell you," she said, as we sat down.

"Did something happen to Harold?"

"No, nothing like that. It's Felix."

"What?"

"Well, yesterday afternoon I went with my mother and my grandfather to the hospital. My grandfather goes for therapy every week and I have to wait for him. It's a drag because I just sit there for about an hour and wait. But who should be there yesterday but Felix. He was waiting for Mr. Havermeyer, who'd been in the hospital for some tests. Felix was picking him up. But Mr. Havermeyer wasn't ready so we had time to talk . . ."

"And?" I egged her on. Rachel can sometimes take a long time to get to the point.

"So naturally we began talking about Harold."

"Naturally."

"And I said how great it was that he could spend so much time with Harold because I can tell how crazy Harold is about him and stuff like that. And, you know how one thing leads to another—so all of a sudden Felix starts talking about someone called Jenny. I asked him who Jenny is. 'She's my little girl,' he says. I mean, I didn't even know he was married! Did you?"

I nodded. "He mentioned it to me."

"Why didn't you tell me?"

"I don't know. I guess I just forgot."

"Kenny! How can you forget something like that! It changes everything!"

"I don't follow."

She sighed and looked at me like I was a fool and

said, "Look, we both know how great Felix is. But when you know he's married and has a two-year-old kid, he's even more fantastic."

"He is?"

"Don't you see—he gives up his weekends with his family just to help his brother!"

"Oh, I see what you mean. Gee, you're right. I guess that is something. I wonder how come he does it?"

"He has to!" she shrieked. "He told me that the reason they took Harold out of the institution was because it was closing down. Harold was going to be sent some place hundreds of miles away and his parents got upset. It would have been so hard to visit him. All these years, they've been visiting him every weekend! So anyway, they didn't know what to do and Felix just had to take over. He found the school for Harold and then the Harrigans' place for them to live. And then of course he promised to help out with Harold."

"I wonder how his wife feels about it?"

"That's just it, Kenny. That's the whole point! His wife sounds absolutely awful. Terrible. Apparently she can't stand Harold. Felix never knew that before. When Harold was in the institution everything was cool with her. She never let on that she couldn't stand him. She probably just tricked Felix into thinking that she was crazy about retards because she wanted to marry him. I mean, who wouldn't want to marry a fantastic, great-looking guy like Felix!"

"Come on, Rachel. How do you know all this?"

"Felix told me. Not in so many words. I mean he didn't come out and say that his wife tricked him into marrying her or anything like that, but that's the feeling I got."

"And?"

"And what?"

"What does it all mean, Rachel? What are we supposed to do?"

"Wait! I haven't told you the worst—I mean the absolute worst part!" She sighed and shook her head dramatically. "Not only can't she stand Harold, but she forbids Felix to take Jenny to see him. She's afraid Harold will hurt Jenny!"

"So that's why his wife is never around."

"Isn't that awful, Kenny!"

"It must be tough on Felix. But I still don't understand what his wife is afraid of."

"Well, when Harold first moved back home, Felix and his wife and Jenny came over. Harold went crazy over Jenny. You know how he is when he likes someone. And Jenny's only a baby. Anyway, he was trying to hug her and kiss her and the kid got scared. She started to cry, so Felix's wife got mad at Harold for scaring Jenny. After that she refused to let Jenny visit Harold. She says it's not healthy for a kid to grow up around someone like Harold."

"She sounds pretty bad."

"Can you imagine? I mean, can you just imagine how much Felix must love Harold to do what he's doing? He is such a great guy. Here he is, probably the greatest guy and his wife doesn't even understand him."

"You don't know that for a fact."

"I don't have to know it for a fact, Kenny. If she loved Felix, really loved him the way he deserves to be loved, she'd help him with Harold. Don't you see—we have to do something!"

"We? What can we do?"

Rachel shook her head hopelessly and sighed. "I don't know. But it's up to us."

"Maybe they'll get a divorce," I suggested.

"I hope so. And Felix gets custody of Jenny. Anyone who can be so heartless as his wife doesn't deserve a great little kid like Jenny."

"How do you know Jenny is so great? We've never even seen her. She could be a screaming brat for all we know."

"I doubt it. All you have to do is listen to the way Felix talks about her to know she's got to be the greatest kid going."

"On second thought, I hope they don't get a divorce. Divorce is pretty heavy stuff and Felix doesn't talk like he hates his wife. What do you think?"

"Oh, I don't know!" Rachel cried out. "Maybe you're right. He didn't say one nasty thing about her yesterday. He mainly sounded sad. He's probably just blinded with love for her. That happens. People do stupid things when they're in love."

Do they ever, I thought to myself.

"There must be something we can do! There has to be!" Rachel exclaimed.

But by the time lunch was over we hadn't come up with a single idea.

"Think about it," she said, as we left the cafeteria.

I thought about it a little because I'd promised Rachel I would, but I didn't have much hope for coming up with a plan to save someone's marriage. I spent most of the time thinking of a way to ask Rachel for a date. I know that sounds incredible. I could talk to Rachel so easily about everything—except us.

She called me that night to find out if I'd come up with any brainstorms and she sounded disappointed when I confessed I hadn't. That bothered me. I didn't want to let her down. When I saw her the next day she was grinning.

"What's up?" I asked.

"I'll meet you at the table for lunch" was all she would say.

That sounded okay with me. She was already there, eating, when I arrived. "I have the greatest idea," she began. "I thought and thought all last night and couldn't come up with a thing—and then, bingo, right in the middle of English this morning, it dawned on me. It's so obvious I don't know why we both didn't think of it before."

"I'll tell you why after I hear it."

"It's so simple! Felix doesn't have to spend *both* days on the weekend with Harold. We can do something with Harold on Saturday. That way Felix will only have to leave his family on Sunday."

"You mean you and me—alone with Harold?"

"Sure. Why not? Isn't that great?"

"I don't know."

"What's the matter with that idea?"

"Nothing, I guess. Except I wonder if Mrs. Havermeyer will trust us."

"Of course she will! We went to the movies with him. Nothing happened. So what's the problem?"

"What are we going to do? Take him bowling maybe?" I asked sarcastically.

"Kenny! That's a great idea!"

I looked at her in disbelief. She'd taken me seriously. "Sure, and maybe we can use Harold as a bowling ball?"

"There you go, stereotyping Harold again," she shot back angrily. That's one of Rachel's favorite expressions. She's always accusing people, me in particular, of "stereotyping" Harold.

"Now wait one minute—you can't ever accuse me of calling Harold a bowling ball before . . ."

She looked like she was going to throw her sandwich at me and I breathed a sigh of relief when she took a huge bite of it instead. She swallowed hard and said, "Funny. Very funny. If you are going to stoop to such childish remarks, which I won't even dignify as witticisms, then I'll do the whole thing myself. I don't need you."

I felt crummy. I didn't think she'd take me seriously. "Hey, Rachel, I'm sorry. Really. I was just kidding."

She looked so sad, I reached out and put my hand on hers and held it, like it was the most natural thing in the world. "Rachel, I'm sorry. I think your idea is super and I want to do it."

"Do you mean that?"

I squeezed her hand and said, "Do you think I'd miss having a Saturday alone with you, not to mention Harold?"

She blushed, which surprised me. And then she said,

"But what about the bowling? I think that's a good idea."

"I don't know. Maybe something else. Can you imagine what it would do for Harold's self-image if we took him bowling and the whole bowling alley ended up watching us like a three-ring circus. It could completely destroy all our weeks of work."

She thought about what I had said and frowned. Then her face brightened and she squeezed my hand. "Wait a minute, Kenny! I just had another brilliant idea! What if other kids came with us. Like Chuck, and Linda and Marie. And maybe you can get Al or Pete to come. And maybe Chuck could bring someone. That way Harold won't stand out."

"How are you going to do that? I just can't see Chuck going bowling with you and me and Harold and a bunch of other tenth graders."

"Leave Chuck to me. He'll come, and I'll convince the others, too. You talk to Felix and get him to convince his mother to let Harold come with us alone. But don't let him know why we're doing it . . ."

She began carrying on and on about the bowling trip and how great it was going to be, but I wasn't listening. I was still holding her hand and I was watching her talk. I thought she was the most beautiful, intelligent, funny, perfect girl I'd ever met. At that moment I knew she was capable of anything—even pulling off this crazy bowling trip.

Suddenly she stopped talking. "Kenny, you're not listening to me!" she exclaimed.

"Of course I'm listening to you."

"You're lying. You have that faraway, bored look on your face."

"No, I swear. I'm not bored. But I was thinking about something else . . ."

"See, I was right."

"Want to go to the movies with me Friday night?"

"What's playing?"

"I don't know."

She smiled and then laughed. "I think I've seen that one and it's terrible. But there's a dance at the Y in Lakeland. Chuck's going. Maybe we can double."

"Fantastic!" I said.

Chapter 13

Instead of going to the dance with Rachel on Friday night I was running back and forth between my bed and the bathroom with a stomach virus I caught from Patty.

I didn't see Rachel all weekend. She called me Sunday night with the news. She'd convinced Chuck to go bowling with us the next Saturday. Linda and Marie were coming, too. And she'd worked out the details with Mrs. Havermeyer and Felix so all I had to do was convince Al or Pete to come—or so I thought.

"But listen, Kenny, we have to spend as much time as we can with Harold this week. I promised Chuck and Linda and Marie that Harold was fantastic. We have to make him as normal as we can by Saturday."

"Maybe you promised too much . . ."

"We're not going to get anywhere if you have an attitude like that!"

"Sorry. Sorry. You're the bowling coach. Whatever you say . . ."

"We're doing this together."

"Great with me," I promised.

And it was. It was fantastic. We spent every afternoon together that week. Of course Harold was with us too, not to mention Mrs. Havermeyer. But it was fun anyway.

At first Harold loved all the attention he was getting. We went to his house every day and did loosening-up exercises. We borrowed my mother's bowling ball and taught him how to hold it. But when we began correcting the way he talked he started to get upset. Rachel could usually make him smile again when she told him how great she thought he was. But then Mrs. Havermeyer started correcting him, too; it was when she picked on his eating habits that he went berserk.

"No! No!" he shouted. "Go away! Leave me alone!" He threw his food on the floor and began screaming really weird things. Not even Rachel could get to him. Mrs. Havermeyer got scared, I guess, and she started yelling at Harold.

"Pick up that food! Are you crazy, Harold? You will scare your friends!"

"Go away!" he screamed.

Then Mr. Havermeyer appeared as if from nowhere. He was standing there, with his arm around Harold, talking to him quietly, telling him everything was okay, telling him how much he loved him and stuff like that. As he talked he slowly led Harold out of the kitchen. After a few minutes the screaming and yelling stopped. But meanwhile Rachel and Mrs. Havermeyer and I were standing in the kitchen. No one said anything or even looked at each other. It was the longest fifteen minutes in my life. I know it was fifteen minutes because I was looking at the clock. I think we were all thinking the same thing, too. I know Rachel and I were. We were thinking about Harold being tied to the tree and how he'd freaked out. And how maybe we had pushed him too far trying to make him normal. He could never be normal, and maybe we were tying him to the tree all over again.

When Harold came back into the kitchen with his father, he was calm again. He said he was sorry and Rachel and I said we were sorry. Mrs. Havermeyer kissed him. Harold began smiling. The crisis passed.

After that we decided to spend our time on his physical appearance—his clothes were awful. Rachel analyzed it this way: "He dresses like a creep. Just like you might imagine a stereotyped retarded person would dress." For once I couldn't argue with her. Harold always wore shiny, baggy black pants. They looked like they were leftovers from an old people's home. His shirts were the same as his father's: thin, white, long-sleeved jobs. They looked okay on Mr. Havermeyer, but on Harold they looked terrible. So did his shoes: black oxfords.

I don't know how Rachel did it, but she got Mrs. Havermeyer alone and convinced her to buy Harold a pair of jeans, a flannel shirt, and work boots. Rachel even convinced Mrs. Havermeyer to wash the jeans a few times before Saturday. And I waterproofed the boots so he could go out without his black galoshes.

Felix must have called me three times that week. He couldn't believe what was going on. "A new Harold. I think it's fantastic! Only you two could have done it. I've been trying to get my mother to let Harold wear jeans for years. It'll change his whole self-image!"

With Harold as set as he would ever be, Rachel and I made detailed plans for meeting on Saturday morning. Chuck was to get to the bowling alley early and reserve a couple of lanes so we'd be ready to play right away. I could just see Harold getting all worked up and freaky if we had to hang around for a half-hour before we got an alley. Al, Marie, and Linda were going to meet us halfway to the bowling alley. That way Harold wouldn't have the excitement of meeting everyone at once.

Friday was a terrible day. I woke up doubting my sanity for letting Rachel drag me into this crazy plan, and as the day progressed my doubts grew more serious.

"It's crazy. It's so crazy I can't believe it!" I exclaimed to Rachel as we were walking over to Harold's after school. "What if he freaks out tomorrow? What are we going to do?"

"He won't," she answered simply.

"How can you be so sure?" I demanded. "Look how he acted the other day."

"Okay, so he was under a lot of pressure. Negative pressure. We're not going to be pressuring him like that. We're just going to be having a good time."

"All the excitement could push him over the brink."

"Possible. Anything's possible." She shrugged casually.

"Well, what do we do if it does happen? Have you even considered the possibility? Has it occurred to you we might have taken on more than we can handle?" I cried.

She stopped walking and looked me right in the eye. "Do you think Felix would have agreed to the whole thing if he thought there was the slightest chance of

Harold's freaking out? Anyway," she added, "we can always hide."

"Funny. Very funny! This is serious, whether you think so or not. After all, we're not the most experienced when it comes to retardates!" I was shouting.

"Okay. If you're so uptight about the whole thing then let's just call it off."

"That's not a bad idea!"

"That's your decision. You can tell Mr. and Mrs. Havermeyer, not me. And you can explain it to Harold."

"Me? Why me?"

"Because you're the one who's chickening out."

"Who's chickening out?" I demanded.

"You."

We stood in the middle of the street, glaring at each other until all of a sudden Rachel began to laugh. "This is ridiculous, Kenny."

I began laughing, too. "You're right! You're absolutely right! What are we doing here anyway? What are we going to see Harold for now anyway?"

"I don't know. To make sure everything's all right."

I dug into my pocket and came up with one dollar and fifty-eight cents. "Let's go to Nino's. I'll treat you to a pizza!"

"Okay!" She grinned.

"Race you!" I shouted, and started running.

"Hey, no fair! You got a head start."

I reached out and grabbed her hand and we ran down the street together.

Chapter 14

Chuck dropped Rachel off at my house at nine forty-five the next morning. We were at Harold's by nine-fifty. The minute we walked in we knew something was wrong. Mrs. Havermeyer was very quiet, which was unusual. And Harold was sitting on the living room couch. He was all dressed in his new clothes, but he was sitting so queerly and he was staring so dumbly that the clothes hardly made any difference. He looked about as retarded as I'd ever seen him. My stomach felt like I was about to take a dive off a one-hundred-foot cliff. From the look on Rachel's face, I knew she felt the same.

"What's the matter?" Rachel was brave enough to ask.

Mr. Havermeyer had come into the room just as she spoke. He hurried over to us and huddled us into the corner of the room.

"What's the matter, you ask! He's scared. That's what's the matter!" Mr. Havermeyer spoke loudly enough so that his wife couldn't help hearing. I don't know if Harold could hear. Even if he could, he didn't seem to be listening.

Mr. Havermeyer glared at his wife and went on. "He's scared that if he makes one silly remark at the bowling alley, a bowling ball maybe will fall on his head. Go ahead, tell him, Rachel, tell him just to be Harold and everything will be all right. Tell him you like him just the way he is, Kenny." There was something gentle about Mr. Havermeyer even when he was angry. He looked at his wife and said, "She wants a normal son. All of a sudden she wants him to act his age when she's been babying him all along."

Mrs. Havermeyer didn't answer. She just stood perfectly still and glared at Mr. Havermeyer.

"Boy, I'd hate to be Mr. Havermeyer when we leave," Rachel whispered to me, as we headed for Harold. And then she began smiling and pulling Harold by the hands. She laughed. "Hey, Harold! What's the story? All set for bowling?"

"I don't want to go. I don't want kids to laugh at me." He looked so sad I almost cried.

"Well, first of all, unbutton your top button," Rachel said, unbuttoning his collar. "Now stand up, Harold. Come on and stand up!" She practically shouted. Rachel has a way of talking to Harold—like they're on stage and the whole world is watching them. Harold loves it. It began working on him right away. He was up in an instant, grinning his heart out.

"Okay, now turn around. Well, would you look at this? I don't believe it, Kenny. Do you see what I see?"

"Aw, come on. Are you really Harold Havermeyer?" I teased.

Harold beamed.

"You look absolutely tremendous!" Rachel exclaimed.

"Out of sight!" I added.

"Come on. Let's go," Rachel said, pulling Harold by the arm. "I got some friends who are just dying to meet you."

Mrs. Havermeyer got Harold's coat, hat, and scarf and started to dress him.

"Sylvia, let the boy dress himself," Mr. Havermeyer sighed.

Mrs. Havermeyer went right on dressing him.

All of a sudden Rachel pulled me aside and moaned, "That hat. We can't let him go out in that hat. He looks so retarded in it."

She was right. Harold's hat was maybe the most retarded thing about the way he dressed. It was a black vinyl job with furry earmuffs and a chin strap.

"What can we do?" I muttered. "She'll never let him out without a hat."

"Give him yours," she said.

"Mine? But it's mine. And it's cold. Besides, I like my hat . . ."

Before I could say another word, Rachel had grabbed the hat out of my pocket. She was holding it high in the air, like a trophy. "Hey, Harold, look what Kenny has for you." And just as Mrs. Havermeyer was about to put on Harold's hat, Rachel plopped my hat on his head.

"That's your hat, Kenny," Mrs. Havermeyer protested.

"It's Harold's now," Rachel said. "Kenny was just dying to give Harold something. Sort of a bowling day present."

"But won't you be cold?" Mrs. Havermeyer asked me.

"No," Rachel answered for me. "Kenny's never cold. As a matter of fact, he hates hats. Right, Kenny?"

"Oh, sure, I hate hats."

"That's funny. I'm sure I always see you in a hat."

"Nope, never!" Rachel exclaimed. "Anyway, we have to hurry. The kids are waiting."

Those must have been magic words to Mrs. Havermeyer, because she suddenly forgot about the hat and began hustling us out the door. She kissed Harold about ten times, and made some worried remark about the possibility of his feet getting wet, at which point Mr. Havermeyer broke in. "So? And if his feet get wet? He'll live. Now, go on, kids—get out of here before my wife gets out the galoshes. And have fun."

Rachel and I hurried Harold out the door, but before we were even down the steps we could hear Mrs. Havermeyer yelling at Mr. Havermeyer. Harold looked back, like he was worried, but Rachel didn't give him a chance to worry long. She began to yakkity-yak the way only she can. I never could understand how she always had so much to say to Harold.

We were halfway down the street when we heard Mr. Havermeyer calling us. He was running to catch up. "Here, treat everyone to an ice cream or something," he said, putting a five-dollar bill into my hand. "Oh, and Harold already has money in his pocket for the bowling."

"No, no . . ." I began to argue.

"Please, Kenny. Take it, eh?"

I could tell he really wanted us to take the money so I smiled and said, "Thanks."

"Don't thank me. I thank you. Now go and have a good time. Hear me, Harold? Have a good time."

And we did have a good time. I couldn't believe it, but everything went off as planned and even better. Linda and Marie and Al were waiting for us. (Pete was working and Al was a maybe until I told him Marie was going.) Right away, I could see there weren't going to be any problems. They were friendly with Harold and Harold was cool. I gotta hand it to him, he was really cool. No hugging and kissing stuff. Just, "Hi, how are you?" Of course, there was no great conversation. After Marie asked him if he had ever been bowling before, and Al asked him about school, there wasn't much to say. Al made one little mistake—he asked him how his rocks were. Al wasn't being nasty or anything. He was just trying to make small talk. Luckily Harold didn't know what he was talking about. He'd stopped playing with rocks. But it was all okay because you could tell Harold was just grooving on being with us. Al and I were acting goofy, throwing snowballs at the girls. We were all laughing, and Harold was holding on tight to Rachel's hand and grinning. Every time I'd ask Harold how he was doing, he'd smile and say, "I'm happy. I like your friends."

We slipped into the bowling alley without hardly being noticed. At one point I fell behind to see if Harold stood out much. He didn't. He didn't walk like a robot anymore except that every so often his right leg would stiffen a little spastically. Even his acne wasn't so bad anymore. Felix had said it had been due to all the greasy food at the institution and I guess he was right. Mostly it was Harold's grinning that gave him away; and, of course, if you listened to him talking for a few minutes. But nobody stared at him or anything. Chuck had the alleys, just as planned, and we began playing right away.

Harold applauded wildly whenever anyone knocked over a pin, even if it was only one. He went crazy when all the pins were automatically cleared away by the machine. But nobody minded. And after a while we were all cheering each other like crazy, too, so it was hard to tell which of us was retarded.

Chuck helped Harold the first time he bowled, showing him very carefully how to hold the ball and swing. Harold listened and then let loose. The ball landed with a thud—it just plopped down, but miraculously it didn't land in the gutter. Slowly, very slowly, it made its way down the lane. It was like slow motion. We all watched, silently—and finally Harold's ball made contact! It knocked over five pins. If there had been any force behind it, it would have been a strike. We all went crazy cheering and congratulating him. I even thought Chuck was going to hug him. The next try, Harold swung harder, but the ball landed in the gutter. We cheered anyway.

It turned out to be a great game. Harold ended up with a score of 61, which wasn't too bad. I gave Harold the five dollars from his father and explained he was going to take us all out for a treat.

"In a restaurant?" he asked excitedly.

"You bet."

"Let's go to the coffee shop."

"Coffee shop it is!" I shouted.

Chuck sort of adopted Harold for the day, and the two of them led the way to the coffee shop. Chuck didn't even seem perturbed when Harold tried to hold his hand. In the end, they linked arms.

Main Street was all set up for Christmas, and we stopped and looked in the windows. "Jingle Bells" was being piped out of one of the stores and when Harold started singing at the top of his lungs, we all joined in. There we were, singing "Jingle Bells," arms linked, as we pushed our way through the crowded street.

Harold insisted that everyone have hot chocolate. So we did. And hot fudge sundaes. We laughed a lot and had a good time. Harold was great. I'd never seen him so excited. And he wasn't too goofy. No worse than any of us. For an unlikely group of people, we really had a good time.

Everyone split after the coffee shop.

"It sure was great seeing you, Harold."

"See you again sometime . . ."

"Merry Christmas . . ."

"Great bowling . . ."

Everyone had something nice to say to Harold. And Harold repeated the same things back.

"We did it! We did it!" Rachel shouted after everyone had left. She turned to Harold and said, "Didn't you have a great time, Harold?"

"Oh, sure. You bet I did. You got nice friends."

"And you're nice, too, Harold!" She threw her arms around him. I hugged Harold, too. And he hugged us and then Rachel and I hugged each other. We were standing in the middle of Main Street, hugging each other. It was so nice hugging Rachel that I hugged her again. And I kissed her. It was all spontaneous. I looked at her and she looked at me and laughed.

"Come on. Let's hurry or Harold's mother will think something's happened to us." She grabbed Harold's hand and then she grabbed my hand and the three of us ran down the street. I guess we ran most of the way to Harold's house—singing "Jingle Bells" and "Joy to the World" and "Santa Claus Is Coming to Town."

Mrs. Havermeyer invited us in. That was the last thing I wanted to do but there didn't seem any way to get out of it. Mr. and Mrs. Havermeyer wanted every last detail of how the day went. Rachel did most of the talking, while I thought about her and how much I wanted us to be alone. I was frantically trying to think of a way to get out of there, when the most obvious solution in the world came to me—the time. All of a sudden I looked at my watch and exclaimed, "My gosh, it's five o'clock already! We better go, Rachel."

Rachel agreed.

We had almost made it out the door when Mrs. Havermeyer began thanking us again and again, and kissing Rachel and smiling at me. I was beginning to feel like I was under attack.

"Man, I thought we'd never get out of there." I laughed as I jumped down the front steps.

We were just outside the front gate when Rachel

cried, "Oh, no! I forgot to call my mother. Mrs. Haver-meyer got me so confused. I better go back and call."

"No! Don't! Then you'll have to wait till your mother gets here. Come on to my house. You can call from there. Maybe my father can drive you home."

"No, that's okay. My mom doesn't mind."

"Well, call from my house anyway."

We started walking down the street. The wind was blowing and I put my arm around her. She put her arm around me.

My house was two minutes away—five if we walked incredibly slow, which we did.

"Did you have a good time, Kenny?" she whispered.

"I sure did. I don't believe it, but I had more fun to-day than I've had in months."

"Me, too."

All of a sudden I was kissing her. We were leaning against a tree about ten feet from my house and the wind was blowing like crazy. I don't know how long we stood there. It seemed like five seconds and it seemed like an hour.

"I think I better go call my mother," Rachel finally sighed.

I held on to her a little longer and kissed her again. "I really like you, Rachel."

"Well, you took an awfully long time showing it," she said. "Think about it. It's been almost two months since I first met you, and it's taken you that long to kiss me!" she teased.

"Well, that's your fault."

"My fault?"

"Yeah, you told me you hated football players."

"I never said I hated them. I said they're stuck-up. And they think just because . . ."

"Don't you ever stop talking?"

"Make me."

So I kissed her again.

"I think you'd better do it again. I feel the urge to talk."

So I kissed her again and again. I thought to myself that I'd never liked anything in my whole life as much as I liked kissing her.

Chapter 15

I thought things would be different between Rachel and me after the bowling trip—a lot different. But it didn't turn out that way. I knew for sure how I felt about her, but I still didn't know how she felt about me. One minute I was positive she liked me and the next I was positive she was laughing at me. For example, I waited for her after English on Monday morning. I hadn't seen her since we'd taken Harold bowling. She walked out of the room with Linda, and acted like she didn't even see me. But she had; she had to have seen me. I was standing right in the doorway.

"Hi, Rachel," I said.

"Oh, hi, Kenny." She smiled and went back to talking to Linda.

Then I made the supreme idiot of myself by saving a seat for her at the lunch table near Mr. Fry. I wasn't too obvious about it. I just dumped my books on the chair and when she passed by I said, "Hi," gallantly lifting up my books.

"Hi, Kenny," she said, and walked right by to sit with Linda.

I was so depressed I went home after school and drowned my sorrows in a bag of Oreo cookies and some Cokes. About three-thirty the phone rang. It was Rachel.

"What's the matter?" she asked. "Are you sick?"

"No, should I be?"

"I didn't know. I thought I'd see you after school. I was looking for you. When you weren't there I thought maybe you were sick."

"I'm not."

"What's wrong? You sound really mad at me."

"Nothing."

"If that's the way you're going to be, I won't call you the next time I think you're sick," she shouted.

"Yeah, well, you know what, Rachel? I could care! I could really care!"

"What's that supposed to mean?" she asked in this really snotty way.

I felt like slamming down the phone. But I didn't. Instead I just let loose about everything I felt. I'm not sure why. It just came out. "It means I'd like to know why you acted like I didn't exist today! It means I'd like to know *now* if Saturday meant anything to you!"

I guess I half-expected her to laugh. But she didn't. She didn't say anything for what seemed like hours. And then she sighed. "Gee, I don't know. I'm sorry, Kenny. I guess I just didn't want the whole school to know about us. And I am helping Linda with the Christmas party . . ." Then all of a sudden her tone changed. Like that—she began getting sarcastic. "What am I apologizing for? I mean just because you kiss someone doesn't mean you're that person's private property!"

That did it. I exploded. "Oh, sure! That's what I

mean. Right! Like it was just a kiss. Like it wasn't all we'd done together. Like I really think I own you! Like I even care!"

Rachel didn't say anything and I got the feeling I was talking to myself. So I shut up ,and listened. She was still there. I could hear her breathing. But she didn't say anything and I made up my mind that I wasn't going to be the first to break the silence. And I wasn't.

"Listen, Friday night, at Linda's party, we can be alone then," she said so softly I could hardly hear her. "It's okay then. Just not at school. I mean, I don't want to—oh, I don't know what I mean," she half-laughed and half-cried. And then she said, "Here I go, running off at the mouth again, not making any sense."

"You have a point there," I said.

She sighed. "You know something, Kenny? I wish you were here to shut me up."

"Yeah?"

"Yeah."

"You know something, Rachel?"

"What?"

"I wish I was there, too."

There was a pause and I squeezed the phone hard, almost as if she was with me, and then she began talking again. "Kenny, I was thinking maybe we can go shopping Thursday for a present for Harold. If you want to get him something. Just something little. I thought it would be nice since Mrs. Havermeyer invited us over Christmas Day."

"Sure, okay, but it's gotta be little. I'm short on

money and I haven't done any Christmas shopping."

"Me, too."

And that was the end of the discussion. Things weren't too different in school on Tuesday and Wednesday. Rachel and Linda were all involved in the party. I played it low-key. But Thursday we had fun shopping for Harold.

We were stifled by only two things: money and the fact that Christmas was just two days away and there was almost nothing left in the stores. We finally bought a fantastic-looking shirt at a fantastic price, considering I hadn't planned on buying Harold anything. After I paid for my share of the shirt, I had thirteen dollars left for presents for my mother, my father, Patty, my four grandparents, and Rachel.

I told Rachel my problem (not mentioning that I was planning to buy her a present). She laughed and said, "Never fear. I'm the original bargain-hunter. It's an old family tradition."

"Yeah, I remember Chuck said you were cheap, but ten dollars for seven people . . ."

"Six. I have this ugly necklace that my aunt gave me for my birthday. It's perfect for Patty and it's still in the box. We can get some perfumey writing paper for your grandmothers. Grandmothers love that. And they have it for ninety-nine cents a box in Woolworth's . . ."

Rachel was right. She was a bargain-hunter. Within an hour I had a scarf for my mother, a wild-looking tie for my father and some fancy soap for my grandfathers. Not too original, but the job was done and there was still forty-one cents left. I treated Rachel to a Coke before she had to go home.

That was Thursday. I spent all Friday afternoon looking for a present for Rachel. She was at Linda's house helping her get ready for a Christmas party that night. I began looking for a present in the department stores, but that was a waste. Everything I liked cost at least ten dollars. So I ended up in one of those boutiques where they burn incense and sell Indian and Mexican stuff. The prices were better, but the saleslady made me nervous. She kept looking at me like she thought I was going to rip something off. Maybe I did look suspicious walking around in circles for about a half-hour in a store that was about the size of a bathroom. Finally the saleslady spoke.

"You must be looking for a present for someone very special. Maybe I can help."

I hate to have salesladies help me. They make me insecure. But at this point I had no choice. I was desperate.

"Who is it for? Your mother?"

"No."

"Your sister?"

"No."

"Your father?"

"No."

She grinned. "Oh, someone *special* then?"

"No, just a friend," I said casually.

"Well." She went on grinning the way only a saleslady can grin. "Is this friend a girl or a boy? It makes a difference sometimes."

I supposed she was right and I told her, "A girl."

"How much do you want to spend?"

I considered forgetting the whole thing, but the saleslady was waiting for an answer so I said, "Five dollars," which included a two-dollar advance I'd gotten from my father on my allowance.

"Oh, she must be a very special girl then?"

I hoped I didn't look as idiotic as I felt.

The saleslady began showing me all these necklaces and stupid stuffed animals from India. I finally ended up with a handmade Mexican belt. I remembered that Rachel had once said that she liked stuff from Mexico. The saleslady even gift-wrapped it for me. I didn't want her to, but she insisted.

"I don't usually do this." She smiled. "But you're such an intense young man."

"Thanks," I muttered, and gave her the five dollars. With tax, the belt came to four eighty-nine. "Keep the change," I said, grabbed the package and ran out.

The package looked very Christmassy, but there was one problem. The saleslady had gone overboard and put the belt in an enormous box. I wasn't about to walk into the party with a big Christmas present and hand it over to Rachel. And I wasn't going to see her before the party since she was helping Linda. So I unwrapped the belt, took it out of the box, and rewrapped it in the same paper. It wasn't so great looking, but it fit into my coat pocket.

I got to the party late because my mother insisted I wrap my grandparents' presents before I left.

"I thought you weren't coming," Rachel said when I walked in.

"Would that have mattered?" I asked.

"It would have. A lot." She smiled and reached out for my hand. Her hair was shining and she had on a great-looking Mexican shirt. I'd seen one like it in the store that afternoon. I was glad I'd gotten her the belt. She looked beautiful. It was dark in the hallway and no one else was there. I put my arm around her and kissed her.

The basement was already jammed with kids. "Like it?" she asked. "The decorations, I mean."

There was a big Christmas tree and wreaths and all kinds of Christmas trimmings. "It's great," I told her. "Want to dance?"

"Sure."

Linda's basement is big, but there were so many kids there it was like dancing in a telephone booth. I like dancing no matter what and so does Rachel. So we danced. We danced all night. About ten o'clock somebody put on an LP with lots of slow music on it and the lights went out. Rachel and I danced and kissed until the lights went on again.

"Sorry, kids, power failure's over for the night." It was Linda's father. And then about eleven-thirty he came back and began announcing whose parents had arrived to pick up whom.

"Remember, kids, Santa Claus only comes to good little children who are snug in bed," Mr. Turner said to us. He thinks he's a comedian. Nobody else does.

Rachel lives only a few houses away from Linda and Chuck came to walk her home. My father was late picking me up, but Chuck and Rachel and I decided to wait outside the Turners' house. Chuck was cool. He moved away from us and began bouncing up and down to keep warm. Rachel and I huddled together.

"Linda's parents are a drag," Rachel stammered, shivering.

The wind was blowing her hair in my mouth every time I tried to talk. It was funny and we laughed. "It's no use talking," I said, and kissed her. She had on some perfume that smelled nice, or maybe it was just her hair.

Then a car drove up. It was my father.

"Be right there, Dad," I shouted.

I dug into my pocket for the present and gave it to Rachel. "Merry Christmas," I said.

Chapter 16

Christmas is a big deal in my house. My grandparents and aunts and uncles and a bunch of cousins come for dinner. My mother is usually a lunatic by ten in the morning, so she wasn't too thrilled about my spending part of the day at the Havermeyers'.

"Today of all days," she said, during breakfast.

"But that's the point, Mom. They wouldn't have invited me if it wasn't Christmas."

"Kenny's got a point there!" my father chimed in. My father claims the only way to get through the insanity of Christmas Day at our house is to laugh.

"Really, Ken," my mother snapped at my father. She thinks the only way to get through the day is to organize every minute like a drill sergeant.

"It's only Christmas, darling. Relax." My father smiled, pouring her another cup of coffee.

I thought she was going to throw the coffee at him and I wanted to get the whole thing settled before my mother flipped out. I had to go to the Havermeyers'. Rachel was going to be there.

"Mom, yesterday you said I could go and now you're finking out."

"It's not fair if Kenny goes," Patty whined. "Then he gets out of doing all his work."

My mother looked at me and sighed. "When do you have to be there?"

"One."

"That's when your grandparents are coming."

I looked at my father for help.

"What if he promised to be back here by two-thirty," he suggested.

"Two-thirty!" my mother cried. "It's ten already. This house is a mess. I'm sorry, Kenny. I just don't see how you can go anywhere today."

"Calm down, Joan," my father said. "All these weeks you've been talking about how wonderful Kenny is to spend so much time with that retarded boy, and now on Christmas you tell him to forget it."

That's how my father always referred to Harold, as "that retarded boy." No matter how many times I told him his name was Harold, my father always called him "that retarded boy."

"I'm not telling him to forget it," my mother sighed. "And besides, that's not fair—using Christmas on me. Why doesn't someone think of poor old Mom on Christmas?"

My father nudged me and whispered, just loud enough for my mother to hear, "I think you're home safe, Kenny. When your mother starts feeling sorry for herself, that's a sign of weakening."

"That's what I like about this house," my mother cried. "We show a united front. One for all and none for Mom."

"I'm on your side, Mommy," Patty said.

"You're not for anyone, brat—you're just against me," I yelled.

"Please, don't the two of you start in! If you two start that bickering . . ." my mother warned me.

"Okay, forget it! Just forget it! I'll call Mrs. Havermeyer and tell her I can't come. But I just wish you'd made up your mind earlier, Mom. Mrs. Havermeyer has probably fixed all kinds of food . . ."

"Just a minute, Kenny," my father intervened. "Does that retarded boy know you're coming?"

"Harold, Ken. His name is Harold," my mother said, and glared at him. "Can't you even remember the boy's name?"

"Remembering him on Christmas is more important than remembering his name," my father said.

"Oh, really!" my mother moaned, and then she said to me, "All right, you can go, Kenny. But you have to help me this morning. And you have to be back by two-thirty. I'll wrap up a box of Christmas cookies for you to take over."

"You don't have to do that, Mom. Rachel and I got Harold a present."

"I know, but I'd like you to give it to Mrs. Havermeyer from all of us. It's just a gesture. I think she'd like it."

"But, Mom, I'm going to feel dumb walking in with a box of Christmas cookies. Why can't Patty bring it to them this morning?"

"I will not!" Patty shrieked. "I don't even know them. They're Kenny's friends."

"Okay, okay, I'll bring them," I said.

My mother had me working like a slave all morning and I was beginning to wonder whether it was worth it, just to go to the Havermeyers' for a few hours. But when I made it (late, of course) Rachel was already there. She was wearing the belt. I knew it had been worth it.

"I love it," she whispered, when I sat down on the couch next to her.

Felix was there, too, and his wife, and Jenny. It was the first time I'd met them. Jenny was cute, but every time I tried to talk to her, she'd turn and run to Felix. Harold thought that was funny. You could see he was crazy about Jenny, but it was clear that he had been given instructions to keep his hands off. He made a point of keeping halfway across the room from her. Whenever she came near him, he'd run. Jenny thought it was a game. I guess it became a game for Harold, too.

Felix's wife, Donna, was another story. She might have been pretty if she'd smiled. But it was impossible to tell since she didn't smile once the whole time I was there. She just sat on the couch, frowning, with a drink in her hand. Mr. Havermeyer did his best to make her smile. He told her every funny story he knew. A few of them even made me laugh. But she just glared and looked more and more bored.

"I think the only thing that'd make her happy is to leave," Rachel whispered.

"I wish she would," I whispered back. Donna Havermeyer's presence was putting a definite damper on the Christmas spirit. Harold was so involved in keeping away from Jenny he couldn't even find time to talk to Rachel. Mrs. Havermeyer was trying her best to serve the food, make sure Harold didn't bother Jenny, and be pleasant to her daughter-in-law as well. Only Mr. Havermeyer appeared to be able to rise above the general misery by laughing and telling funny stories. I'd never seen him so talkative but I think it was because he kept on filling his glass with wine. Mostly Rachel and I just sat on the couch and watched. Felix tried to keep up a conversation with us, but his mind was on too many other things.

Felix asked me to help him get some things from the kitchen. As soon as we left the room, he said, "Kenny, I'm sorry for the lack of cheer. I know it's Donna. She just doesn't understand Harold. I don't know if she ever will," he added sadly.

"That's okay, Felix. Really. I'm having a good time."

"It's been hard on her since Harold's come home. I guess she never expected that he'd be so much a part of our lives. And, well, I guess she doesn't think that it's good for Jenny to be around Harold so much. I know that's absurd, but fear is a hard thing to deal with sometimes, Kenny."

I felt embarrassed having Felix apologize for his wife to me. Luckily Rachel came to get us.

"What are you guys doing out here! Come on, Santa Claus is coming!" she exclaimed.

Mr. Havermeyer clapped his hands for attention, and began in a dignified voice, "Ladies and gentlemen. We have here today our very own Santa Claus!"

"That's me!" Harold shrieked with delight.

"Then go on, Santa, and get the presents," Mr. Havermeyer urged.

Harold was so excited he almost knocked over the

Christmas tree as he dug underneath it for presents. He was funny and everyone laughed, except Donna, of course. Jenny was having a great time. She kept on following Harold and getting the presents all messed up. That got Harold uptight and finally Felix held Jenny on his lap. Harold relaxed.

"Ho, ho, ho! Merry Christmas!" he shouted.

"Presents! Presents!" Jenny shouted, trying to get off her father's lap.

Harold laughed. "Santa got presents for Jenny." Then he went through this whole show of reading out the names on the presents and handing them out just like a regular St. Nick. Except he couldn't read so he gave everyone the wrong presents. Rachel and I were really surprised. We got three presents each. Records from Felix. I got a new hat from Mr. and Mrs. Havermeyer, and it was a nice one, too. Rachel got one of those six-foot scarves. I was glad Rachel had thought of getting Harold a present. He flipped over the shirt and put it on right away.

Then he gave Rachel and me our presents. He'd saved them for last and they were the best of all. He'd made them himself in school: a leather wallet for me and a little wooden box for Rachel. "For your diamonds and jewels," he told her.

"It's beautiful!" Rachel exclaimed, kissing him. "I didn't know you did things like this in school."

"Yeah, I've never had such a great-looking wallet!" I added. Harold was so happy, he kissed me.

Chapter 17

Rachel came up with a New Year's resolution—effective immediately, as of the day after Christmas. It wasn't so much a resolution as a plan. She dubbed it "The Socialization of Harold Havermeyer." She told me about it over the phone on Christmas night. At first I didn't say anything. I wasn't sure I understood what she meant.

"Did you hear me?" she asked.

"Yeah. But what does it mean?" I asked cautiously.

"In plain English it means that we include Harold in as many things as possible. It means we treat him just like any other kid."

"That's what I was afraid of," I exclaimed. "It means you're nuts, Rachel. I'm not going to drag Harold all over with us."

"But that's just the point, Kenny. We don't have to drag him any place. He just comes along. Look, you can hardly tell he's retarded anymore."

"That depends on who he's standing next to." I thought that was funny.

Rachel didn't. "What's the harm in trying?" she asked.

"Only the waste of the Christmas vacation. We did have plans. Remember? Skating. A movie. Who knows what? I don't want to have a retard shadowing us."

"Kenny!" she shrieked. "I can't believe you said that!"

To tell the truth, neither could I. I'd thought things like that lots of times, but I made a point of not letting Rachel know. It just slipped out this time. So I tried to cover it up. "I was only kidding. I like Harold. You know that . . ."

"Yeah, well, I don't think it's so funny. I think this is really important. We have plenty of time to do things, but Harold . . . I mean, look at him. Look what he was and look what we've done for him. He was so fantastic today. That really makes me feel good. That's important. It's so important, Kenny. We can't give up on him now."

"I'm not giving up, Rachel. We can still do things with him on Saturdays. I'm all for that."

"That's easy. But it's not enough. It's like giving up, Kenny. It's selfish. It's like saying I've done as much as I'm gonna do and anyway, he's just a retard and he doesn't know any better. But he does. And you'll see, the more we involve him the more normal he'll get."

Rachel can be very persuasive.

"Okay," I sighed.

"You don't sound like you mean it," she insisted.

"Come on, Rachel! What do you want?"

"I want you to mean it. It's important. It says something about the kind of person you are if you're really willing to give something of yourself."

"Okay! Okay!" I shouted as enthusiastically as I could. "I mean it! I love it! I can't think of anything I'd rather do than spend my Christmas vacation carrying out the Socialization of Harold Havermeyer!"

We both laughed.

"Thanks again for the belt. I love it."

"I'm glad."

"But how come you didn't tell me you were getting me something? I don't have anything for you."

"That's okay."

"No, it's not!"

"Okay, it's not. Buy me something, then."

"I can't. I spent all my money."

"Well, you can treat me to a soda tomorrow."

"I didn't know I was going to see you tomorrow."

"Well, you are," I said. "That's my Christmas present."

"Okay, I'll meet you at your house and then we can get Harold. And then I'll treat you both to a soda."

"Some Christmas present," I moaned.

"See you tomorrow, Kenny."

"Hey, Rachel. Want to come to Fred Murphy's New Year's Eve party?"

"I thought you'd never ask." She laughed.

"You could have asked me."

"Next time I'll know better."

"Hey, Rachel—let's bring Harold, too!"

"To a New Year's Eve party!" she exclaimed.

"Just testing."

"You're a nut!" She laughed.

"Thanks! Coming from you that's a compliment."

The Socialization of Harold Havermeyer turned out to be not so bad after all. It wasn't hard to convince

Mrs. Havermeyer that we could take care of Harold. Rachel's word was law. Besides, Harold turned out to be not so much of a pain as I thought he would be. Mostly he just tagged along with us or in front of us or behind us. And, because of him, I got to see Rachel every day during vacation.

We took him to get pizza and one night Felix got us tickets for a basketball game. Harold didn't understand the game, but he loved the noise and the crowd and he cheered like crazy. Another day, Mr. Havermeyer treated us to bowling and a movie. The only absolutely impossible thing was skating. Harold was a complete zero on the ice. But other than that, he was okay.

But by New Year's Eve I had had my fill of Harold for a while. I couldn't believe that Rachel and I were really going to be alone—without the shadow. My mother drove me to Rachel's about seven-thirty. It was a drag having to be dependent on parents to get anywhere, but I'd be sixteen in a few months and then I could start driving during the day. My mother left me at Rachel's. Her parents wanted to meet me. Then Chuck was going to give us a lift to the party.

Mrs. Simon answered the door. "Kenny." She smiled. "I'm really glad to meet you at long last."

I know that sounds phony but she said it like she meant it. The first thing I noticed about Mrs. Simon was the way she looked—just like Rachel, or I should say Rachel looked like her mother. They both had the same smile.

"Come on in. Rachel's still getting ready."

Mr. Simon was sitting in the living room reading.

"Mike," Mrs. Simon said, "this is Kenny."

"Kenny!" he exclaimed, standing up to shake my hand. It was a warm, friendly handshake and I felt I was with people who liked me.

Just then Chuck came in with a soda. He was covered with paint. "Hi, Kenny. Want a Coke?"

"No, thanks."

"Chuck, would you tell Rachel that Kenny's here," Mrs. Simon said. "And you'd better get cleaned up."

"Sure thing." He walked into the hall and screamed up the stairs, "Rachel! Kenny's here!"

"I could have done that," Mrs. Simon sighed.

I heard someone running down the stairs and then Rachel appeared.

"That was fast," her father teased.

"That's because I didn't want to leave Kenny alone with you guys." She grinned. "You see, Kenny, they know all about you and they've just been dying to meet you because they can't believe you're as great as I tell them you are!" She laughed and grabbed hold of my hand.

"That's true," her mother said.

"It's also true that nobody can be as great as Rachel claims you are," Chuck added.

"Chuck!" Rachel cried, and she blushed.

I thought she was the most beautiful girl I'd ever seen. I wasn't even embarrassed by Chuck's remark. I was walking on air.

"What time am I supposed to chauffeur you to the party, anyway?" Chuck asked.

"Eight," Rachel said.

"Then I'd better get ready."

"Aren't you already ready?" She laughed.

"Yeah, it's a masquerade party and I'm going as Michelangelo," Chuck said. "Next time, *you* paint the basement."

"For what you're getting paid, I might!"

"Ha! That'll be the day!" Chuck teased, and hurried out of the room before Rachel had a chance to get the last word in.

"You might as well make yourself at home," Rachel moaned. "It takes Chuck an hour to get ready for a date when he's clean." And then she looked suddenly angry and said, "Honestly, Mom, I don't understand why he didn't stop painting earlier. I told him the party started at eight."

"Your father can drive you," Mrs. Simon promised, and that seemed to soothe Rachel.

"I have an idea!" Mr. Simon said. "Since this is New Year's Eve and your mother and I aren't doing anything—except opening some champagne and waiting for you kids to get home—how about if we open a bottle now? You drink champagne, don't you, Kenny?" Mr. Simon laughed.

"I never have," I admitted.

"Oh, Daddy, you talk like we have champagne all the time!" Rachel interrupted.

"Well, this is the big year for the two of you, right? What do you think, Barbara?" he asked his wife.

"Sounds great to me, if your parents wouldn't mind, Kenny?"

I hadn't the slightest idea whether or not they would

mind and I didn't care. "Oh, no, they wouldn't mind,"
I said.

"Daddy! You're such a nut!" Rachel laughed and
kissed him. "Can we really have champagne?"

"I think there are two bottles. And I don't think
your mother and I can drink them both."

"I'll get the glasses!" Rachel volunteered.

"And the champagne," Mr. Simon said.

"Is it in the refrig?"' she asked.

"It better be." Mrs. Simon laughed.

"Come on, Kenny. I need your help," Rachel said.

I followed her into the kitchen. "Your parents are
nice," I said.

"I like them." She giggled. "And I love champagne.
I've had it at weddings. I can't believe my mom and
dad are opening a bottle for us. I bet they had this
whole thing planned. I bet they bought this bottle just
for us!" She opened the refrigerator and took out the
champagne. "Hmm, good stuff." She smiled.

"How do you know?"

"I don't." She laughed. "But it's French and it says
Brut."

"I'll remember that next time I'm buying champagne."

"There's a bag of potato chips in the cabinet," she
said. "Want to get them?"

"Where? What closet?"

"That closet. There," she said, pointing to a door.

"I can't see. You'll have to guide me."

"Oh, Kenny!" She laughed and pulled my hand. I
pulled her toward me and kissed her.

"Not here!"

I held her for a second and said, "Did you really tell your parents about me?"

"Don't let it go to your head!"

"It already has. Have I told you how beautiful you are?"

"Not here!" she insisted, and pulled away.

"I can't help it!" I moaned.

"Try. You're a grown-up boy."

"That's the problem."

She threw the bag of potato chips at me, and showed me where the glasses were.

"I think we should get Chuck down if we're having champagne," Mrs. Simon said, when we came back to the living room.

"Do we have to?" Rachel sighed. "It'll only take him longer."

"We have to," her mother said.

Rachel went to the stairs and screamed for Chuck. "We're having champagne. Want some?"

Chuck was down in a minute, in his bathrobe.

"Here I am, dressed for the occasion. If I'm not appropriately attired it's because I didn't know what the occasion was."

"New Year's Eve, idiot!" Rachel said.

"New Year's Eve comes every year and we've never had champagne before!" he said. "I thought maybe we were drinking to Kenny and me for the great football year we had. Oh, God, I don't like to think about it— I've played my last game for Baldwin High."

"If you're this drippy when you're sober," Rachel said, "what are you when you're drunk?"

"Ah, only Marcia Krebbs knows for sure!"

"Then I think I'll drink to Marcia Krebbs," Rachel said. "She may need it."

Mr. Simon poured the champagne. "If you don't mind, Rachel, I'll make the toast."

"Watch it, Kenny," she whispered. "I think this was all planned and I think it's going to be mushy. My father can get very mushy sometimes."

"Do you think you could manage to stop talking long enough for me to make a toast?"

"I'll try, Daddy."

"Okay—here we go!" Mr. Simon exclaimed, as he raised his glass. "To Rachel and Kenny—two nice kids."

"And to all the nice things they've done with Harold," Mrs. Simon added.

I half-expected Chuck to make a wise remark, but he didn't. Instead he said, "I'll drink to that."

We all touched glasses and drank the champagne. It's strange, but I didn't feel the least bit embarrassed.

Rachel and her parents and I sat and talked while Chuck was getting ready. I thought we might spend the whole time talking about Harold, but we didn't. Mr. Simon asked me about football and for the first time Rachel didn't groan. We talked about school and Mr. Simon told some funny stories. Everything made me laugh. We were all laughing and having a good time. There's a nice, easy feeling about Rachel's family. I don't think there was a moment's silence. It was easy to see where Rachel and Chuck got their senses of humor. I was having such a good time I almost didn't feel like leaving when Chuck came down.

"That champagne is great stuff," I said, when we got outside. I put my arm around Rachel and pulled her close to me.

"Feel warm and tingly inside?" she asked.

"Yeah."

As we got in the car, Chuck said, "No necking below the neck under the influence of French champagne."

"Just drive, Charles," Rachel said.

Chapter 18

Fred's party was by invitation only and everyone came with a date. Fred's parents were home, but they were nowhere to be seen and stayed that way all night. The party started out to be fantastic: low lights, slow music, and nobody was talking to anyone except their dates. It was the first time Rachel and I had been alone like this with only one thing to do—be alone, dance and make out and have the most fabulous night of my life.

Then around eleven-thirty some kids crashed the party. They were loud and obnoxious. One guy had a guitar. He began playing some hard rock and the lights were turned up. Somebody started passing out beer, and the room suddenly exploded into noise and movement.

"I think I liked it better before," Rachel sighed.

"Definitely." I caught hold of Fred and asked, "Where did all these kids come from?"

Fred was too drunk to care. He stared at me with a glassy-eyed look and said, "I don't know but they're outtasight."

I looked for Pete, who was still making out with his date. I tapped him on the shoulder. "Want to split?" I asked.

He looked at me in amazement and then turned to his date and said, "Want to split?"

"Where?" she said.

"That's a problem," I said. "Any ideas?"

"No. I guess I'll stay."

"If you come up with an idea . . ."

"Yeah, sure, Kenny," Pete promised, and I got the distinct feeling he wanted me to disappear. I went back to Rachel.

"What's up?" she asked.

"I don't know. I'm not in the mood for something like this. The whole party's changed thanks to those creeps."

"He plays the guitar nice."

"Yeah, if you're in the mood."

"And you're not?"

"Yeah, if the lights were low and if we were alone and if the guitar player was just a shadow in the moonlight."

"That's what I like about you, Kenny. You're so romantic." And then she began sniffing.

"What are you doing?" I laughed.

"Pot. Somebody's got pot!" she exclaimed and sniffed again.

I sniffed. "You're right," I said. I didn't tell her, but I'd never smelled pot before.

"You smoke?" she asked.

"You?"

"I have. Last year I was into it for a while. I wonder who brought it? I think they're passing it around. Want some?"

I remembered trying to smoke cigarettes in Perry's car. I felt dumb telling Rachel I didn't smoke, but I knew I'd feel even stupider if I tried and began choking. I think she guessed from my silence that I didn't want to smoke.

"Hey, Kenny, that's okay with me if you don't smoke," she said, and put her arm around me. "I mean, it's no big deal either way. I can take it or leave it. Besides, I'm high just being with you."

I'll never forget how I felt when she said that to me. I loved her so much. I wanted to tell her. Instead I kissed her and said, "We gotta get out of here."

That's when I heard something that made me nauseous—Phil's laughter. It had to be Phil's. I'd know his laughter any place. He was the last person I wanted to see that night.

I grabbed Rachel's hand and headed for the door.

Phil saw me right away. He was passing a joint to the guitar player.

"If it isn't my old pal, Kenneth Shea. Hey, pass the joint to my friend Kenny," he shouted.

"No, thanks," I said.

"Come on, Kenny. The football season's over. Don't tell me you're still in training?"

"Ignore him," Rachel whispered.

Phil tried to stand up, but he fell back and began laughing wildly. "Somebody help me!" he screeched. "The floor just moved on me. Hey, Fred, what the hell kind of floors do you have in this house?"

I didn't laugh, but everyone else sitting in the circle around Phil thought he was hysterical.

"It's the Mental Lovers! Somebody help me over to the Mental Lovers!" Phil cried out. "Maybe they want a joint of their very own. I'm feeling generous tonight. It's New Year's Eve. Come on, Mental Lovers—you want a joint of your own?"

Phil passed around another joint. "Pass it on to my friend Kenneee!" He laughed.

"They're stoned," Rachel said. "It's no use talking to them. Anything you say will just make them laugh more."

We went into the hall where it was dark and we were alone. "I don't know why I'm letting him bother me like this," I said.

"Look, he's trying to cut you down, make you feel stupid. But he's the one who's stupid, Kenny. Anyway, I have a surprise."

"You're beautiful, Rachel."

"Do you want to hear my surprise?"

"Sure."

"See, I worked out this deal with Chuck. I usually hate parties, so in case this one turned out to be a drag . . ."

"Which it is."

"Chuck said I could call him and he'd come and get us."

"Then what?"

"He's doubling with a friend of his and they're having a very private party at his friend's house, and he said we could come."

"You're kidding?"

"Would I kid about a thing like that?"

"But Chuck's your brother. I mean, I wouldn't do something like that for my sister."

She sighed and held my hands. Then she said, "Chuck and I have been really close since Laurie died. I tell him everything. He's the greatest guy I know."

"What about me?"

"Well." She laughed. "You're a close second."

"Thanks. Thanks a lot."

She called her brother and he and his date, Marcia Krebbs, picked us up in about ten minutes. For a girl with a name like Marcia Krebbs, she was very attractive.

"Are you sober?" Rachel asked when she saw Chuck.

"Not really." Chuck laughed. "But don't tell Dad."

"Don't worry," Marcia said, "I'm driving." And then she sniffed. "Somebody's got grass here."

"You're kidding!" exclaimed Chuck. "Show me the way."

"Come on, Chuck. That's why we're leaving," Rachel said, grabbing hold of his arm."

"What's the matter with you two? Square or something?"

"It's not the pot," she sighed. "It's the people with the pot. They're obnoxious."

"Maybe we can just sneak a joint on the way out?"

"It's Phil Canady's grass," Rachel said.

That seemed to sober Chuck up. "Oh," he said. "Forget it."

"Who's Phil Canady?" Marcia asked.

"A creep," Chuck replied.

"Oh," was all Marcia said.

Chuck's exclusive party was great. He and Marcia were in one room. His friend and his date, whom Rachel and I never got to meet, were some place else; and Rachel and I had the living room all to ourselves.

Rachel said she had to be home by one-thirty and Chuck and Marcia drove us both home. As I got out of the car, Rachel whispered to me, "I meant to tell you— you have definite advantages over Chuck."

"So do you."

Chapter 19

After that things got better and better between Rachel and me, if that's possible. We were going together and everybody knew it. We ate lunch together, studied together, tried to be together almost every Friday and Saturday night, and mainly spent as much time together as we could. Even Phil's infantile remarks stopped bugging me. I guess he realized I didn't care anymore because after a while he stopped. It was like he disappeared from my life.

The biggest problem was finding a place where we could be alone. Rachel's house was off limits till her mother came home from work, which wasn't until about six. If we went to my house after school, Patty hung around us like a leech and my mother became obsessed about us keeping the door of any room we were in open at all times.

Then Al and Marie began going out together in the middle of January. We doubled a lot for a while. Al's parents almost always went out on Saturday night and we all would go to his house. But Al and Linda broke up in February and there was no place for Rachel and me to be alone.

Besides that, we were still spending a lot of the time on weekends with Harold. Rachel insisted on that. It didn't bother her—we were just one happy threesome—but it started to bug me.

March came and it rained every day. I've never seen anything like it. The ice and snow melted and the ground was mud. Mud every place. Everybody was going batty with the weather and we needed a party. One day after school I invited Pete and Al and a few guys over and Rachel invited some of her friends—including Harold. That day started a routine that lasted until spring. A couple of afternoons a week, we'd all meet at my house because it was closest to school and sit around and listen to music. My mother never seemed to mind as long as we cleaned up. And she pretty much left us alone when a lot of kids were over, so Rachel and I could fade away into a corner piled high with cushions. Then it was just Rachel and me. And the world was beautiful.

Harold came almost every day. His big thing was dancing. He had turned into a fantastic dancer. He never got tired. And when nobody wanted to dance with him, he'd just dance by himself. Most of the time he was pretty quiet. Although some days he'd come in talking his head off, hugging and kissing everyone. When he got like that, we'd push him away and tell him to shut up. He never seemed to mind. He was happy as long as he was with us.

I met Felix one afternoon as I was passing Harold's house.

"Hey, I hear you and Rachel are really making it together," he teased.

"What? How'd you know?" I asked, feeling the red crawling up my neck.

"Harold." He laughed.

"What'd he say?"

"He told me, very confidentially, of course, that you and Rachel make out all the time."

"Yeah, he said that?" I answered him as coolly as I could.

"Sure. Why not? Don't you think he notices?"

"I guess. I never thought about it."

"Some retarded people even get married and have kids. Just because their brains don't function normally doesn't mean they can't love and feel just like you and me. Hasn't Harold told you about his girl friend at school?"

"No! He's got a girl friend?"

"Her name's Evelyn. And she's got long black hair and she's the prettiest girl in the school. At least Harold thinks so."

"No kidding. So old Harold's on the make! Maybe I should give him some pointers."

Felix laughed. "Maybe he could give you some pointers!"

I think maybe Felix realized that I wasn't too comfortable with this subject because after that he started talking about basketball and school. But I couldn't forget what he'd said to me about Harold and sex. I tried to imagine Harold making out with a girl, but I couldn't. It was impossible. What girl would want to be kissed by a retard? Especially before Rachel and I had socialized him. I tried to see it from Felix's point of view. I tried not to be turned off by the whole idea.

Felix was right. After all, he knew more about retarded people than I did.

I didn't tell Rachel about it at first. I couldn't. But I was becoming more and more aware of Harold watching Rachel and me. It seemed like he was always gawking at us. And when he wasn't gawking, he was touching Rachel, holding her hand or hugging her and telling her how much he liked her. I was beginning to take a distinct dislike to Harold, not because he was retarded, but because he was always around . . .

"I don't think you should let Harold touch you all the time," I said to her casually one day.

"What are you talking about?"

"Harold. He does happen to be a member of the male sex and he does happen to be almost nineteen. Didn't it ever occur to you that he might, well . . . you know . . ."

"No, I don't know . . ."

"Of course you know! You know exactly what I mean," I said angrily. I could tell by the silly grin on her face that she was teasing me. She didn't say anything. She sat there, grinning.

"I'm talking about Harold and sex! I mean, he's not exactly a monk!" I cried in exasperation.

"How do you know?" she demanded. "Do you and Harold sit around and discuss your sex lives?"

"Don't be ridiculous! Felix told me."

"Felix told you what? That . . . that Harold makes it with some cool-looking chick every Saturday night!" She laughed.

"Would you shut up and listen to me for once!" I shouted.

"No, I won't listen to you at all as long as you're shouting. Besides, I'm relieved to hear about this. I was worried about his sex life . . ."

"What! You were worried about his sex life!"

"That's what I said. You don't have to repeat it."

"Well, do you think it's normal? I mean can *you* imagine making out with a retard?"

"Now you're being ridiculous. Of course not. But I think it's normal for him to feel just like you and I do."

"How would you like it if he felt that way about you? Which he probably does."

"I think you're jealous, Kenny," she said perfectly seriously.

"Jealous! My God! I don't believe you said that! My God, the idea of being jealous of a retarded person— it's, it's gross! All I said was I think you should think about letting him hold your hand all the time."

"He does the same thing to you and to everyone else who's nice to him."

"But he does it more to you. You can't deny that!"

"You are being so ridiculous, I'm not even going to continue discussing this with you. It's very obvious that you're just transmitting all your hang-ups about sex to Harold."

"My hang-ups!" I shouted. We were sitting in the park and there were all these mothers taking care of little kids and I was beginning to notice that some of them were staring at us. So I laughed sarcastically and said to Rachel, "Speak for yourself."

"Shut up," she snapped, and stood up. "I really can't stand you anymore." And she walked away.

We didn't talk to each other for four days. I was

miserable. The only thing that made it bearable was that Rachel looked just as miserable as I felt. Finally we agreed to sit down and calmly discuss the whole thing. Which we did. I admitted that I couldn't stand having Harold around us all the time, except I said it more diplomatically, like I loved her so much I couldn't stand sharing her with Harold. I also ended up apologizing. She agreed that we could cool it with Harold a bit. I thought that she should have apologized too, but under the circumstances I didn't push it.

Chapter 20

Harold wasn't the same good old Harold to me after that. It was dumb. I told myself it was dumb. Harold wasn't doing anything different. He was still goofy, always ready to shake hands and hug you half to death. The difference was me. He was bugging me. Everything he did bugged me. I couldn't even stand the thought of being around him sometimes.

Then as if in answer to my prayer, Harold got the flu. His mother kept him out of school for three weeks and, even after that, she wouldn't let him budge after school until the weather warmed up. It was easy to get out of the habit of having Harold around, thinking about him and including him. It seemed like we all forgot about him. Even Rachel. And it was great. Rachel and I got along like never before. Everything everybody ever said about spring and love was true. And passing my driver's test made it even better. I had scheduled it for April 10, my birthday. "We're not supposed to do this," the tester said when it was over, "but since it's your birthday, I'll make an exception. You passed, kid."

"That's the best birthday present anyone ever gave me," I told him.

"Enjoy it." He smiled.

I did. My mother was pretty cool about letting me use the car. In exchange for doing errands, I could use it whenever she didn't need it, which pretty much solved the problem of where to go to be alone.

"It gives you such a sense of freedom, having a car," Rachel said to me one day.

"Can you imagine this summer? We can go to the beach. Who knows where? Even at night. It doesn't get dark until almost nine in the summer."

"What about a job? I thought you had to get a job this summer."

"I am. I have to. How can I get a car without a job?"

"You're not really serious about getting a car, Kenny?"

"I am. It probably won't be for at least a year. I mean, I don't want to buy some old heap that keeps breaking down."

"Have any ideas about a summer job?" she asked.

"Nope. You?"

"As a matter of fact, I do. You know the programs the town runs for little kids—you know, the swimming programs and stuff?"

"Sure. That's where I learned how to swim."

"A friend of Chuck's worked teaching the kids swimming last summer. He said it was a great job. The hours are only eight-thirty to twelve-thirty and the pay isn't bad. All you need is a life-saving certificate. Do you have one?"

"I think so. You?"

She nodded. "I was also thinking," she said, grinning

slyly, "since the coach is in charge of the summer recreation program and since you and Chuck are two of his favorite people, well, if the two of you talk to him, maybe he could help us get the jobs."

"Brilliant! What a brilliant idea!"

"It goes without saying—it was mine!" She laughed.

I talked to the coach the next day about the jobs.

"I can't promise you anything, Kenny. Those are the most popular jobs because of the hours. But if you and Rachel go down to the recreation department and fill out applications, I'll see what I can do."

"Thanks."

"But I'm not promising."

"I know."

"What about something else, if the swimming doesn't work out? They need instructors for the camps and the baseball and softball teams."

"Could Rachel and I work together?"

"Boy, you don't ask for much, do you, Shea?" The coach laughed. "Just the most-sought-after summer jobs and now you want to work with your girl, too. Well, I'll see."

"When can we find out?"

"Early June. I'll let you know as soon as I know, okay?"

I had the feeling that the coach was going to come through. Rachel and I didn't even apply for any jobs except swimming instructor. After all, when things are looking up, they're looking up. I didn't think we had a problem in the world.

Then one bright beautiful May morning I got a

letter. Nobody ever sends me mail and I could have done without this, too. It was an invitation to a bazaar at Harold's school. I laughed when I read it and threw it away. The prospect of going to a retarded bazaar and being surrounded by hordes of retardates wasn't my idea of a way to spend a Sunday afternoon. I mean, we hadn't even *seen* Harold for about six weeks.

Rachel felt differently. "I think it'll be fun," she told me.

"Funny is more like it."

She glared at me.

"It was only a joke."

"You really don't like retarded people," she said.

"Let's not get into this," I sighed. "Harold's okay. I guess they all are. They're just not my thing."

"Well, *I* think it would be an interesting experience to see Harold's school. Even you might learn something."

"I guess I have no choice then. It's Harold's school bazaar . . . or death . . ."

Rachel began attacking me and shrieking, "Ohh! Sometimes I hate you, Kenny!"

"Stop! Stop! I'll go! I promise!"

She stopped attacking me and said seriously, "Don't do me any favors. You don't want to go—so don't. I don't care in the least."

The last thing I wanted was a big deal over Harold, and I could tell Rachel was taking this thing seriously, so I kissed her and said, "I want to go. I swear. Not to see Harold's school. Not to see a bunch of retardates. But to be with you. Although I'm not sure why!"

That made Rachel smile and she put her arm around me. "I do." She laughed. "Because I'm beautiful and intelligent."

"Well, you'll at least be the most beautiful and intelligent girl at that bazaar."

"That's me!" She laughed. "One step above Harold's girl friend. You got good taste, Shea!"

Harold's school was a lot nicer than I'd expected, although I'm not sure what I expected. It didn't look much like a school. It was in a big old house that had been renovated. We got there early so that Harold could give us the grand tour: from the kitchen to his classroom to the woodworking and leather shop to the sewing room.

"Too bad we don't have some of this equipment," I said, admiring the woodworking tools. "I mean it's kind of a waste here . . ."

"Kenny!" Rachel sounded shocked.

I laughed. "How come you always fall for it!"

The tour lasted for about a half-hour mainly because Harold showed us everything from the freezer in the kitchen to the silverware drawer to the shaving stuff in the men's room. By the time we returned to the main room, the school was jammed to overflowing. I'd never seen so many retarded people and I couldn't help staring. A lot of them were weirder than Harold. Much weirder.

"Look at him," I whispered to Rachel, and pointed out this guy with a head like a Martian. "He should have a lot of brains in that head," I went on. "But I bet there's not a one."

Rachel kicked me hard.

"Ohh," I moaned. "I forgot. No sense of humor today."

"Cut it out, Kenny," she pleaded. "Somebody might hear you."

All of a sudden Harold grabbed on to both Rachel and me and began pulling us steamroller style through the crowd. "Kathy! Kathy!" he shouted. Harold's voice boomed above the general insanity and Kathy heard him. She was his teacher. We'd heard all about her from Harold.

As soon as Kathy reached us, she smiled and said, "Don't tell me. You're Rachel and Kenny."

"And you have got to be Kathy!" Rachel exclaimed. "Harold talks about you all the time."

Kathy laughed. "And all I hear about is you!"

I didn't say anything because I couldn't help staring at Kathy. Harold was always saying how pretty and nice she was, but I'd formed an independent picture of what a teacher of the retarded had to look like: short, fat, and middle-aged with fuzzy hair. Was I off base! Kathy was in her early twenties and everything Harold said about her was true.

"Is something wrong?" she asked me.

"No," I said stupidly.

"You have to get used to Kenny," Rachel said sarcastically. "He stares a lot. He can't help it. He was born with this terrible disease . . ."

"Are you serious?" Kathy asked.

"No, that's just Rachel's sense of humor," I added quickly.

Kathy and Rachel got a good laugh out of that and then Kathy went on to tell us what super-terrific kids we were. "You two must be the first thing Harold thinks about when he wakes up and the last thing at night. Just about everyone here knows you. Harold's quite a talker. This is my first job teaching the retarded, but the other teachers say that Harold's development has been very impressive. His family's told us you two have done it all. Do you know that when he first came here he was in the lowest group? He's moved up three groups since then . . . Oh, there's Bob Heller. He's the big boss around here. I know he wants to meet you."

Kathy introduced us to Bob Heller and all the other teachers. Everybody was nice and friendly, especially Kathy. I think I would have worked hard enough to move up into Kathy's group, too, if I were Harold!

Then Harold introduced us to Evelyn, his girl friend. She was very shy and Harold, almost cave-man style, had to drag her to meet us; and then she wouldn't look at us. She just kept her head bowed and giggled. She wasn't too weird-looking as retardates go, and considering his choices, Harold hadn't done too badly.

He was gentle and understanding with her once he'd dragged her over to us. "These my good friends, Evelyn. Say hi. They're Kenny and Rachel. I bet they like you, too, 'cause you're nice and pretty."

All Evelyn would do was giggle.

"Kathy, make Evelyn say hello!" Harold finally cried in exasperation.

"I can't make Evelyn say hello," Kathy explained. "But I know that she's happy to meet your friends, Harold." She touched Evelyn gently on her arm and said, "Aren't you glad Harold brought his friends, Evelyn?"

Evelyn looked at Kathy and nodded. Then she looked down again and giggled.

"Evelyn's just shy. We can't all be so outgoing and friendly as you, Harold," Kathy went on.

Harold grinned proudly. "Yes, I am friendly," he agreed.

"Why don't you go and get Evelyn something to eat," Kathy suggested. "Or better yet, why don't the two of you get something for all of us?"

Evelyn nodded. Harold took her hand. "Be right back in a jiffy," he assured us, and the two of them disappeared.

"Harold is really a character!" Kathy laughed. "And I'm not just saying this, but I think of all the kids in my class, Harold is my favorite. He adds some zip to the day."

We spent the next ten minutes or so exchanging Harold stories, which was kind of fun. Rachel and Kathy did most of the talking, mainly because I was afraid to—Rachel always took Harold so seriously that I had become conditioned not to make a joke out of anything that had to do with Harold or retardates. At first I was amazed to hear Rachel laughing about him, but I guess she figured that if Kathy, a regular retardate teacher, could laugh and make fun of Harold's crazies, so could she.

Then Harold reappeared with Evelyn and some food and a horde of retardates who wanted to meet Rachel and me. I must have shaken hands with every one of them at least twice and half of them hugged me till I thought I would suffocate. I guess we really were some kind of celebrities to them and Harold was the hero of the day. After all, he had brought us.

Chapter 21

The bazaar was much better than I'd expected. I could even say I'd had a good time, but it was hardly a momentous occasion. Not so for Rachel. It got her started on retardates again and for the next week all I heard about were Kathy and the bazaar and how great they were.

It didn't bother me at first. I figured Rachel would get over it. I thought that if I played it cool, she'd get the idea that I'd rather not talk about Harold and retardates all the time. I knew that she and Kathy talked a lot on the phone, and that was fine. They'd hit it off from the very beginning. Besides, I liked Kathy. I thought her approach to retardates might be healthy for Rachel. But the more Rachel talked to Kathy, the more involved she became with Harold and retardates again. Sometimes I felt as if she talked to me only to give me a blow-by-blow description of her conversations with Kathy.

I guess I'd really had it one Saturday morning when I tried to get Rachel on the phone for an hour and a half, and it turned out she'd been talking to Kathy. Rachel and I had planned to go hiking, but Friday night my mother decided she needed the car, so I had to cancel. Then Saturday morning my sister woke up feeling sick so my mother decided to stay home. She said I could use the car. That's when I tried to call Rachel for an hour and a half.

When Rachel explained she'd been talking to Kathy, I blurted out, "What is this with Kathy? Do you have to spend your life talking to her about retards?"

"What's that supposed to mean?" she snapped.

"It means I'm sick of Kathy and the retarded school!"

I thought Rachel would start screaming at me, but she didn't. She was silent for a few seconds, and then said, in a super-controlled voice, "If that's the way you feel you should have told me."

I took a deep breath and said, "Look, I'm sorry. Really. It's just nerve-racking to get a busy signal for an hour and a half. I just wanted to tell you that I can have the car and we can go hiking. We could have been there already if you hadn't been on the phone."

"Gee, I'm really sorry, Kenny," she replied sarcastically. "But how am I supposed to know that? I mean, my whole life doesn't revolve entirely around you."

"Come on, Rachel. I said I was sorry. Forget what I said about Kathy and retardates. I'll pick you up in fifteen minutes. We can still go."

"I can't. I made other plans," she answered.

"But why? We had a date."

"You broke it."

"I didn't break it. I just said we couldn't use the car. I figured we'd still get together."

"But you didn't say that, Kenny. How was I supposed to know?"

There was no sense in pushing the point. I could tell she didn't want to see me and I had the distinct feeling her new plans had to do with Kathy. So I sighed and said, "You going out with Kathy?"

"Yes" was all she said.

"Yeah, okay. I'll see you. Call me if you find time in your schedule . . ."

"Hey, Kenny, wait a minute. I'm sorry, too. I really am. Let's go hiking tomorrow. And I'll get all my retardate talk over with today. Promise." She laughed. I knew she was sorry, too.

"That's okay, Rachel. I don't mind. I just don't want anything to come between us."

"It won't. I promise. Anyway, I'm glad you told me how you feel. God, I must have really been boring you talking so much about Harold's school! But I promise. No more. Okay?"

"Yeah, sure—that'll be the day!" I teased.

"I mean it, Kenny."

"Hey, Rachel."

"Yeah."

"I love you."

Rachel didn't bring up the subject of retardates again after that, although she talked to me about Kathy and I knew she saw her. Still, it bugged me every time she mentioned Kathy. It wasn't anything big, just one of those little annoyances that sometimes made me feel like I was going to explode.

Maybe it sounds crazy, but I think I was jealous of

what Rachel and Kathy shared. It was a part of Rachel I didn't know and probably never would. It was the not knowing that made me scared.

But what was I afraid of? Rachel loved me.

Then why did it bother me when Rachel saw Kathy? Why did it drive me up a wall when I'd try to call Rachel and I'd get a busy signal?

Luckily, it was only when I was apart from Rachel that I worried. When we were together, all my fears vanished. If anything, I was more in love than ever. I couldn't see her enough. Be with her enough. Talk to her enough. Look at her and hold her and kiss her enough. I didn't want to share her with anyone ever again.

The end of the school year was coming fast—too fast. Term papers and finals seemed to be crashing all around me. There was that promise I made to my father about doing better, not to mention the fact that exams and I don't get along too well. The minute I sit down for an exam my mind freezes and I feel like I'm going to puke. During the last month of school I felt myself getting crazier and crazier. The only thing that could save me was Rachel—Rachel and only Rachel.

We were studying together one night at her house and I told her that, but not in so many words. Then I said something I'd been thinking of saying for a while. The time seemed as right as it ever would be. "I've been thinking. Why don't we call off Saturdays with

Harold for a while. I have so much work to do, I really need Saturdays to study."

To my amazement she agreed without any argument. "It's funny, I've been thinking the same thing."

"Ah, great minds . . ." I began, and leaned over to kiss her. And then I said, "Let's put off all studying till Saturday."

"Come on, Kenny, be serious. We have to study."

"But this is studying. Love is life," I said philosophically. "We're studying for life—the real thing!"

She frowned and pulled away. "Honestly, Kenny. I can't study with you at all. We *never* get anything done."

She seemed so serious that I got up and walked across the room. "Look, I'll sit here and you stay there. I won't even look at you for fifteen minutes."

She still wasn't smiling.

The phone rang and Mrs. Simon called in, "Rachel, it's for you."

I read for the first five minutes she was gone; but for the next ten minutes I fumed. I knew she was talking to Kathy. It had to be Kathy. Kathy was the only person Rachel would speak to for fifteen minutes when we were together.

When she came back she was smiling, which annoyed me even more. Kathy could make her smile but I couldn't.

I didn't mean to say what I said next. It just fell out. "I suppose that was Kathy on the phone."

She glared at me and answered, "Yes. Anything wrong with that?"

I thought for a second and decided not to push it

anymore. I said, jokingly. "Hey, no, nothing! I just wanted to show off my tremendous deductive powers."

She still wasn't smiling. "Kenny, don't push me about Kathy."

"Come on, I was kidding . . ."

"No, you weren't. I know you don't mean to, not really, but you have been pushing."

There was something so sad about her voice and her face. She wasn't mad. She was hurt and the last thing I wanted to do was hurt her. I went over to her. "You're right. I'm sorry. Never again, I promise."

I kissed her and she kissed me and that was the end of the studying for the night.

When I saw her the next day I said, "Let's study together tonight."

She shook her head. "It's impossible. We just never get any studying done. We're both going to end up flunking."

I tried to change her mind, but she was insistent, especially about Saturdays. Saturdays, she said, she needed to study alone.

I got less done alone than I did with Rachel. I told her that. I told her I needed her inspiration but she was really serious about studying separately. Soon it seemed that every time I wanted to see her she was studying. Nobody studied as hard as she did. The only time we got together was during lunch and Friday or Saturday night. Sometimes we studied together for a little while on the lawn behind the field at school. It's a nice place to study. Lots of grass and big maple trees. Lots of kids study there.

One day I said to her, "Rachel, I just have to see

you alone more. This is crazy. Studying is one thing, but all you're doing is studying." And then I said something which shocked even me as I heard it coming out of my mouth. "But I bet you find time for Kathy."

She stared at me and gasped. "I don't believe you said that."

"Forget it. I don't believe I said it, either. I didn't mean it. It's just all this studying and never being alone with you. Come on, let's take a study break. Let's go for a walk or maybe I can get the car." I put my arm around her.

She pulled away and said, "Not now, Kenny. I *really* have to study."

This time there was no mistaking her response. It was a definite turn-off. I know I shouldn't have said what I said about Kathy. It was incredibly dumb; but it still didn't deserve the response it got. I felt so numb inside I didn't know what to say or do, so I opened my book and stared at the page for about five minutes.

Finally she put her hand on mine and said, "What's happening, Kenny?"

I could tell she felt miserable, too; and knowing that made me forgive her.

"It's the pressure of studying, that's all. Come on, we need a study break."

"I don't know." She shrugged. "I don't feel like it. I think I'll just go home. Chuck said he was leaving about four. I can get a ride with him."

I thought about Rachel and me a lot that night. That's all I thought about and I convinced myself that I was making a big deal over nothing. We were all under a lot of pressure. Anyway, it'd all be over soon and then vacation. Two beautiful months just to have fun. Nothing was going to ruin that.

The next day I was sitting in the locker room getting ready for gym and going over some math proofs in my head when the coach came over to me. "Kenny, we decided on the swimming instructors last night. You and Rachel have the jobs if you want them."

"Thanks, coach! That's great. I really needed news like that now."

"I thought it might give you a lift," he said.

I couldn't wait to tell Rachel, but I wasn't going to see her until lunch. I was meeting her behind the field under the maples. Our usual place. She was already there by the time I arrived.

"We got it! We got it!" I shouted.

"Got what?"

"The instructors' jobs."

"Oh" was all she said. Her face wasn't exactly the picture of joy I'd expected.

"Oh what? Oh good? Oh bad?"

She looked at me and smiled. "I'm sorry, Kenny. I'm glad. I really am."

"You don't sound it."

She grabbed hold of my hand and I sat down next to her. She squeezed my hand hard and I thought she was going to cry.

"What's the matter? Is something wrong?"

"Oh, God, Kenny! Why can't things ever work out the way you plan?"

"Hey, what's wrong?" I asked again. I thought

something terrible had happened to her. But it hadn't. Something terrible was about to happen to me. I knew it even before she said it. I could tell because I felt her pulling away from me again.

"I'm not taking the job," she said.

"What? Why?"

"I have another job . . ."

"But we planned it, Rachel. We had the whole summer worked out."

"I know, Kenny. I'm sorry. I really am. It's just that this other thing came up and I really want to do it."

"Is it a big dark secret or can you tell me what this other great opportunity is?"

"Kathy got me a job," she said nervously.

"I should have known!" I said angrily.

"I knew you'd react like that," she said defensively.

"How am I supposed to react?"

"You could understand. You could at least try to understand . . ."

"Understand what? That some dumb job with Harold is more important than me—than us?"

"It's not with Harold. It's with a bunch of little kids—kids like Laurie. They remind me so much of Laurie. There's this one little girl . . ."

"Hey, wait a minute—have you already started or what?"

She blushed and said, "Well, Kathy works with these kids on Saturdays . . ."

"Oh, sure, now I see it all. And you've been going with her. That's why you agreed to break off the thing with Harold and that's why you couldn't study with me. I'm distracting but retards aren't."

She reached out and touched me. "I'm sorry I lied to you, Kenny. I wanted to tell you the truth. I was going to . . ."

I felt more angry and hurt than I'd ever felt before. I felt like yelling and shouting and punching someone or something. It was hot but now I was sweating like I'd just run the mile in a hundred degrees. I stood up to leave. I had to get away from there.

Rachel pulled me back. "Wait a minute. Listen to me. It's important. I want you to understand. I had a retarded sister. She was a part of my life and I loved her and I can't change that. I want to work with these little kids. I just want to."

"So what am I supposed to tell the coach? There are plenty of kids dying for these jobs and he gives them to us and you turn it down," I said angrily.

"I'll tell him. He won't care. It just means somebody else gets the job. Nobody's being hurt."

"Nobody's being hurt!" I practically choked on the words. "Nobody's being hurt."

"Kenny, you're talking like I'm doing something to you. I have the right to take any job I want. You don't own me. I can do what I want. Just because we talked about the swimming job doesn't mean I'm bound in blood to take it."

"I never said you were. But at least you could have told me you were thinking of not taking it. At least we could have talked about it. At least you didn't have to lie to me."

"Why? So you could have told me that I was a jerk to want to work with retarded kids?"

"I wouldn't have said that. I never said that. I went along with you all the time with Harold. Didn't I?"

"That's just it—you went along. Well, thanks a heap . . ."

"I'm so sorry, retardates will never be my thing," I said angrily. "But they're obviously yours. Yours and your friend Kathy's."

"What's that supposed to mean?"

"It means that everything was fine between us until Kathy came on the scene."

"God, Kenny, sometimes you're so stupid! I can't stand it!"

"Then don't!"

"I knew you would react like this. I just knew it! Why can't I work with a bunch of retarded kids and still go out with you?"

"Yeah, you can. You could—if you were normal. If it didn't take over your whole life—which it will."

"Stop it, Kenny. Just shut up!"

"You better believe it, Rachel. But before I do I want you to know something. If you take that job it's over. Not because I want it, but because it'll happen . . ."

"Yeah, well, you know something, Kenny. That's fine. That's perfectly okay with me!"

She grabbed her books and left.

For two days I was so angry at Rachel I didn't care that it was over between us. And it was over this time for good. I guess I realized that when the coach told me Rachel had turned down the job. That's when I stopped feeling angry. I was almost relieved. I didn't need Rachel. Our relationship had become a bore. Sure there had been good times, but basically it was a bore. Maybe it had always been a bore. What kind of relationship can two people have if it's based on retardates? That was a good one. It made me laugh. The Socialization of Harold Havermeyer. It sounded like the title of a movie that was doomed to obscurity even before it was released. Rachel was a jerk. She deserved the Harolds of the world. That's what I told myself, but I knew it wasn't true because I hurt so much—deep down inside I hurt whenever I saw her or thought about her.

Chapter 22

Somehow I got through finals and everything else I had to do but I didn't do too great in anything. I barely passed the chemistry final. I ended up with an overall average of 78. My father blew his stack.

"It isn't acceptable, Kenny. That's all there is to it. How do you expect to get into a decent college with marks like that?"

"I guess I won't."

"Oh, that's a good attitude, Kenny. You told me that after the football season you'd do better. Maybe you should just forget about the football next year."

"Yeah, maybe . . ." I sighed, and I meant it. I didn't care about football. I didn't care about anything.

"Take it easy on him, Ken," my mother said.

"That's the problem. We've always been too easy on Kenny."

"It's hard when you're sixteen and you break up with your girl friend," my mother said.

"Maybe he shouldn't have been so involved with her to begin with. Involved with football, with that retarded boy, with his girl friend—with everything except what really matters right now and that's his school work!" my father screamed on and on.

"You're wrong!" my mother cut in angrily. "What

Rachel and Kenny did with Harold was as important as anything he could have done in school."

I knew she was trying to help. I knew she meant what she said, but I was sick of hearing about how important Harold was—like the whole thing, everything Rachel and I had had together, mattered only because of Harold.

I exploded. "I wish Harold never existed! Dad's right. I wasted this whole year. It was a zero. Nothing!"

My mother put her arm around me and said, "I know you don't really feel like that, Kenny. It's just the hurt. It'll pass . . ."

"Hurt? What hurt? You think Rachel hurt me?" I laughed. "I'm glad it's over. And she wasn't the one who ended it. It was mutual. Believe me—it was mutual!" I shouted and went to my room.

About fifteen minutes later my father came up and sat on my bed. I knew I was in for one of his father-son talks that he prides himself on. Except this time I also knew my mother had put him up to it because he began by talking about how he remembered his first girl friend and how I should feel free to talk to him about anything, anything at all; but I knew for sure that he was too angry about my grades to care about my social life. So after he finished with the man-to-man, heart-to-heart, understanding bit, he gave me the real reason for his coming up. "Have you given any thought to summer school? You know, bring up the marks, especially the chemistry."

I hadn't expected that. It hit me like a punch in the stomach. It made me sick. "Summer school!" I said as calmly as possible. "That's the last thing I could do, Dad. You gotta believe me. It wouldn't do any good. I've had it with school. I really have. And besides, the coach got me this job. I couldn't do both."

He looked at me with a deep, soul-searching look and I didn't know what to expect. He wrapped his arm around my shoulder and squeezed hard, "Okay, Kenny, I won't push you. But next year . . . next year you gotta do better."

"I will, Dad. I promise."

"And the football. I didn't mean what I said about the football. I know how important that is to you. But maybe you could cool it with the girls." He smiled. "I mean, it doesn't have to be so hot and heavy."

"You have a deal!" I grinned, feeling strangely elated.

He started to leave and then turned around. "Kenny, don't ever knock what you and Rachel did with that retarded boy. You and Rachel wouldn't have gone on forever."

Those words did something. I wasn't elated anymore. I had a knot in my throat and my eyes burned. I nodded to my father and he left. And all of a sudden I began to cry.

I had two weeks to kill between the end of school and the beginning of my job. Two weeks to kill and nobody to kill them with. I could have hung out with some of the guys, but I didn't feel like it. I mostly stayed in my room and listened to records and read and tried not to think about Rachel. That was the worst. I kept on thinking about her. So I concentrated on the negative aspects of the past year. And that made me mad. It wasn't so bad when I was mad at her. It was when I realized how much I missed her that the time dragged and I'd get that numb feeling inside and I'd slam my fist into my pillow over and over again.

I woke up on the Fourth of July feeling almost happy. Only two more days till the job started. There was a big celebration at the Memorial Field on the Fourth. I didn't want to go, but my parents were having a cookout, an adult thing, and I knew if I stayed home I'd have to serve the food and make conversation with their friends. I couldn't think of anything I wanted to do less, so I went down to the Memorial Field.

The Fourth is a big day in Baldwin. There are races and swimming meets and one of those traveling amusement parks. For a dollar you can get chicken, French fries, and corn on the cob. And at night there's a band and dancing before the fireworks. It's also pretty easy to avoid people you don't want to see since Baldwin has the biggest Fourth of July celebration in the county and people come from all over.

I got to the field about three and watched the swimming meet for a while. It was a typical Fourth of July day—hot and humid. I bought three Cokes in an hour and tried to find a place that wasn't in the sun. I took off my shirt and thought about going home to change into some cut-offs. It felt like an oven inside my jeans.

But it was too hot to walk home so I decided to get another Coke.

Suddenly I heard my name being called. I didn't have to look to find out who it was. Instead I began planning an escape route through the crowd; but I wasn't fast enough. I felt hands clinging to me in the way that only Harold can cling.

"Kenny! Kenny! How are you, Kenny!"

I pulled free of him and he stepped back and held out his hand to shake.

"Hi, Harold," I sighed, and didn't shake his hand.

"I here with Rachel!" he announced, grinning from ear to ear.

I looked past him just in time to see her at the very minute she saw me. She was walking with a retardate on each arm along with Kathy and some other teachers I'd met at the bazaar.

"Harold!" she called. "You can't go so far ahead. It's too easy to get lost."

Harold grinned and said, "Look who I found. I found Kenny!"

"Hi, Kenny." She smiled.

"Hi."

In an instant I was surrounded by the retarded brigade.

"I gotta tell you something," Rachel said in a way that I knew meant she had something to say that she didn't want Harold to hear.

"Sure," I said, happy to escape.

"Stay with Kathy," Rachel told Harold, and we walked a few feet away.

"I just thought you'd want to know that Mr. Haver-meyer had a stroke last week. He's in the hospital and they don't know if he's going to make it."

"Gee, that's tough. I didn't know. How's Harold tak-ing it?"

"He doesn't know. His mother told him that his fa-ther just went away for a while."

All the time Rachel was talking she was looking right past me. She could have been talking to people standing behind me. And all the time I was looking at her. She was hot and sweating and her hair was plas-tered against her head. Her T-shirt was damp with sweat and it clung to her in wet splotches. It was all I could do not to grab her and kiss her. It was all I could do not to say, "Let's get a Coke and talk. Let's forget everything and start all over. You go with your re-tardates, but let's still see each other."

But I didn't say any of it. I didn't say anything. We stood there in silence for a few seconds until one of the teachers came over and said, "Hey, Rachel, we're taking them over to the rides."

"Okay, Carl." She smiled. "I'll be right there."

There was something about the way she smiled at Carl and the way he smiled at her that made me hate him.

She turned back to me and said, "Anyway, I just thought you'd like to know."

"Yeah, well, thanks for telling me."

"I gotta go."

"How's the job?"

"It hasn't really started yet," she said. "It starts

Wednesday. I'm just doing this because Kathy asked me if I wanted to."

"Yeah, that's nice," I said. I had meant to say it like I meant it, but instead it came out sarcastic.

She frowned at me and said, "Typical."

"I didn't mean it that way."

"It doesn't matter," she told me, and left. "Carl, wait up!" she shouted. And he waited for her.

Chapter 23

Suddenly an arm fell around my shoulder and a head smashed into mine. I turned to meet the attacker and came face to face with Phil. He was standing there, grinning at me like an imbecile.

"What the hell!" I shouted.

"It's my old buddy boy, Kenny!" He laughed. There was something funny about the way he was grinning and the way his words slurred together. At first I thought he was drunk, but I was close enough to smell if he had been.

"Why don't you and me talk, Kenny, pal? I'm serious. I heard you and Rachel split. I'm sorry, man. Really sorry. You two had a thing going. I could never see it, of course. But each to his own," he said solemnly. He wasn't laughing. I had the feeling he did just want to talk.

"Yeah, well, that's the way it goes," I half-laughed.

"Kenny, I'm going to say something and I want you to know that I'm serious. And what I'm gonna say is this: I'm really sorry about everything that's happened. I mean, you and me were pals. You were the best friend I've ever had. I miss you," he almost cried. There he was, staring me right in the face, eyeball to eyeball, with his eyes filled up with tears. "Do you believe me?" he pleaded.

"Sure I believe you, Phil," I said, because I was afraid if I said I didn't he would sit down on the ground and cry. I couldn't figure out what was going on, but if Phil needed me so badly he was on the verge of tears, I couldn't fink out.

"Want to go some place and talk?" I asked.

"Great idea! How about my house? Nobody's home and we can put on the air conditioning. Just like old times!"

We went to Phil's house. It's not far from the field. Besides it was good to get away from the crowd and the heat. We immediately emptied the refrigerator of everything worth eating and went to the family room. Phil turned on the air conditioning and I sat down in the big bean bag. It felt good to be back in Phil's house. Like old home week.

"Make yourself at home," Phil said. "I'm gonna get us some more goodies!" and he exited in a flourish. He was back in a few minutes holding up three joints. Phil was stoned. I don't know why I hadn't realized it earlier.

"How about a few pokes, pal?" He grinned and lit up, then inhaled deeply. "Presto! Bingo! All your problems vanish."

"When are your parents coming home?"

"They're away, away, away!" he shrieked, and collapsed laughing against the wall. "It's just Perry and me all weekend. Why they trust us, I'll never know." He laughed some more. "And Perry's out with his girl friend. So we ain't got no problems."

He handed me the joint. I still didn't know how to inhale. "It looks like a pregnant cigarette," I said.

That broke Phil up.

"Come on, Kenny. Aren't you gonna smoke?"

"Yeah, sure," I said. It was now or never, I decided, and put it to my lips and drew in. Instantly I began choking until I thought I'd suffocate. My eyes were tearing and Phil was hysterical. He had fallen into a lump at my feet.

"Kenny, baby! Don't tell me you never smoked before!"

"I refuse to answer on the grounds that it might incriminate me," I said, and tried to take another drag. I choked again. Phil pulled himself up and said seriously, "We have to go about this scientifically. Once you get the hang of it, it'll be a breeze. First you got to hold your lips tightly around the joint and take it in just a little. Then swallow."

I don't know how long I was sitting there or how many joints Phil kept on producing. It seemed like an endless supply.

"Where do you get all this?" I asked.

"Perry. He has a friend who has the most beautiful pot plants you ever saw."

"Since I've never seen one, I'll take your word."

Phil got so stoned after a while he stopped smoking, but he refused to give up on me. My eyes and throat were so hot they began to feel numb. I was ready to forget it. Another failure. I couldn't even smoke grass. Then all of a sudden I got an uncontrollable desire to laugh. And I laughed and laughed and laughed. Phil began jumping up and down, screaming and yelling. "It worked, Kenny! It worked! You're stoned! You're stoned out of your mind!"

I'm not sure how long we stayed at Phil's house. I guess until the food ran out. I'd never felt so hungry in my life and food never tasted so good. Then I felt so full I thought I was going to throw up. But I didn't. We listened to records for a few years until Phil said, "I got the greatest idea. Let's go back to the park. We gotta watch the fireworks. Do you realize how fantastic the fireworks are going to be stoned? They're going to be fantastic! Absolutely fantastic!"

"Okay, if you say so. Let's go."

I tried to get up, but I couldn't. My body felt like lead. "I can't move," I moaned.

"I know. I can't, either."

So we sat for a while longer. All the time Phil kept talking about how he couldn't think of anything better than watching the fireworks except maybe making out, which made me think of Rachel.

I think Phil was reading my mind because he said, "How far did you get with her?"

"Rachel?"

"Who the hell else would I mean?"

"I dunno."

"So tell me."

I thought about it for a while and said, "That's a very personal question, Phil."

"Yeah, I know."

"And it's none of your goddamned business," I added.

"Aw, come on, Kenny. The next best thing to making out is talking about it."

"I'll tell you this much—my relationship with Rachel was much more than just sex."

"I don't believe you."

"It's true. It was more of a merging of minds," I said, feeling very philosophical.

"No kidding. Hey, that's beautiful. Except for one thing—I don't believe you!" And he broke out laughing.

After he stopped laughing we didn't talk for a while. I kept on thinking about Rachel. Finally I said, "You know something, Phil. I think I really loved her. I never told anyone that. But I really loved her. I guess I still do."

"Hey, man, your feelings are safe with me. You can tell me anything. Anything at all."

"You're a friend, Phil. The best friend I've ever had. You know, I feel bad when I think about the way I treated you."

"Forget it. It was the time, man. That's all. You were in love. I understand."

I talked about Rachel for what seemed forever. And I cried some, too. I can't believe all the things I said that night. Things I didn't even know myself. All the time, Phil just sat across from me, staring. I don't think he was even listening to me. It didn't seem to matter.

Then all of a sudden I stopped talking. My mouth and mind felt like mush. I lay back in the bean-bag chair, listening to the music. The music drifted through my mind and body; it became a part of the way I felt. I didn't know what group we were listening to. I couldn't even zoom in on the words, only the beat. It all seemed so right, so beautiful, like Rachel and me. I wanted her with me so badly that my body ached.

I said out loud, "She's a crusader. She's like a Joan of Arc. And that's beautiful. Really beautiful."

"Who?" Phil asked in a faraway voice.

"Rachel."

"The untouchable one."

"Yeah. Untouchable. Like a high priestess." I began to envision Rachel sitting high on a golden throne, dressed in diamonds, emeralds, and rubies.

Phil lit up another joint. He took a couple of drags and passed it on to me. Immediately I began floating. Higher and higher . . . I was too high. I was cold. I was falling. I breathed in deeply and shivered. "This stuff is terrible," I cried to Phil.

"Go with it, man."

"I can't. I'm scared."

Phil laughed bitterly. "You don't trip on grass. Kenny. Be cool. Just go with it. Enjoy the high. It's the best thing that'll happen to you. Believe your old pal. Let yourself go for a change. Forget that uptight chick. She played you for the proverbial fool, pal. Nobody could have done that to you when we were together."

I heard his words and I thought I should be angry; I didn't like to hear him talking about Rachel like that. But getting angry seemed like too much of an effort at the moment. Instead I tried to focus on his face and said, "That was crummy, Phil. But I'll let it pass. I forgot it already."

"Yeah, sure. Forget it. It's only words. It's only the words of the best friend you'll ever have. She did a number on you, man; and you did one on me."

"I didn't" was all I could manage to say. I didn't want to argue. I could hardly get my mind together long enough to come up with a coherent thought, much less a sentence.

Forget Phil, I told myself. You're finally stoned and you might as well enjoy it. Do as the man says. Go with it. I blocked Phil out of my mind and concentrated on Rachel. I tried to recapture the picture of her on the throne, to recapture the way I felt when we were together and everything was right.

Rachel was just beginning to come clear when all of a sudden Phil was standing in front of me, screaming. "Reality, man! Do you know what reality is?"

Rachel was gone. Phil was there. I couldn't stand losing her. I couldn't stand Phil's screaming. I began to get up. "I'm leaving," I told him.

He grasped on to my arm and said frantically, "Okay, okay, I'm sorry. I didn't mean what I said about Rachel."

Staying was definitely easier than leaving, so I fell back into the chair and said, "Okay, I'll stay. But you can't come on like that again."

Phil nodded and went to turn over the records. He sat down on the floor, directly in front of me and after staring at me for a few seconds he began talking again. "I knew this would happen one day, Kenny. I've been waiting for it. Ever since I heard you and Rachel split."

"Waiting? For what?"

"For you and me to get back together again. We both got guts and brains, Kenny. It's gonna sound corny and I don't mean it that way, but you and me are a team. There isn't anything we can't do together."

Phil stopped talking and I felt that I should answer him. This was a new Phil. A Phil I didn't know. He was almost begging me for friendship and I didn't know what to say. I thought to myself that I'd been crazy to come here. I'd been suckered in by Phil again. There he was, ready to pick me up on the rebound. It was crazy. Too crazy. I couldn't think straight. I was going around in circles. Almost a year had gone by. Rachel had gone by. Maybe—maybe I could be friends with Phil again. But one thing I knew for sure—for absolute certain—Phil and I could never be a team again. Not on his terms, anyway.

Maybe Phil gets psychic when he's stoned, because suddenly he said to me, "I know what you're thinking, Kenny. You're thinking we're not a team anymore. You're on your way to be a football hero and old Phil here is nothing but a pothead."

"Hey, no . . ."

"Well, maybe I am a pothead, but I'm not blind and I'm not stupid. I know the score, Kenny. Give me credit for that."

"Sure, Phil. I do."

"And you know why I know the score? Because a little thing called reality smashed me over the head with it. It pulled me on the right track. You live in a dream world, Kenny. And I used to, too. The New York Giants and *The New York Times*. Dreams in futility."

I shook my head. "I don't think so."

He laughed bitterly and said, "Well, let me tell you a story, Mr. All-American . . ."

174

"Hey, cut it . . ."

"Okay. Okay. You're right. No sarcasm. I just want you to know something."

"Sure. Shoot."

"See, when you were trying out for the football team, I was doing my thing, too. Believe it or not, I went to the first meeting of the so-called newspaper, where everybody's supposed to get acquainted, where us lowly but eager sophomores are supposed to be 'encouraged to participate'—supposed to be led on to new and greater heights by the upperclassmen and all that bull! Upperclassmen! Some pimply-faced creep on an ego trip ran the whole show. He stood there telling *me* what was coming down because he was a senior! So I raised my hand, stood up, and asked this creep if he was for real . . ."

"What did you do that for?"

"Because nobody but me had the guts to tell him where to get off!" Phil stood up. His voice was getting louder and louder, and he began to wander around the room.

"That crud had the nerve to tell me that he was going to be elected editor this year, that's who he was, and he didn't think he wanted people like me on his staff."

I thought to myself that if I was this pimply-faced creep I wouldn't want someone like Phil on my staff, either, but I kept still.

"Hell, Kenny, I couldn't believe it. 'His' staff! I mean the guy couldn't talk his way out of a roll of used toilet paper, much less edit a newspaper. So anyway, I said I was willing to take him on right then and there, have a straw vote, him against me for the editorship."

"You did?"

Phil was really getting into his story. He was on stage and I sat there, watching him, mesmerized. I could see the whole scene—Phil and the pimply-faced senior. Phil against the world.

"Yeah. I challenged him to make a speech. The both of us, about how to run a newspaper. He laughed at first, but I let him know I was serious. Then some heavies said he should take me on. They were laughing. They thought he could put me down."

"What about a teacher," I interjected. "Wasn't a teacher there?"

"Nah, his wife was having a baby, I think. He had told this creep to run the meeting. Anyway, our future editor finally said yes, but I'd have to go first. No sweat, I told him. I made a great speech, Kenny. I wish you could have been there. I remember thinking at the time, I wish Kenny was here. It was probably the greatest goddamned speech those half-witted kids will ever hear and all the time this pimply jerk and his friends were making wisecracks, laughing, trying to make me sound like a jerk. But they couldn't because I knew what I was talking about. I didn't give in. I kept on talking till I'd said what I had to say and then I walked out. I told them they didn't deserve to have me as their editor."

Phil lit up the joint again and we sat smoking in silence. I was getting more and more stoned. Going with it, as Phil had said, feeling crummy that I hadn't been there to help him, feeling crummy that I'd been too involved with football to even find out what had happened. The higher I got, the crummier I felt until all of a sudden I realized—that's exactly what Phil wants: to make me feel guilty, to put me on a guilt trip. Crazy. Crazy. Crazy, I thought. I had too many other feelings about Rachel and me to cope with. I couldn't get hung up over Phil.

"Have another drag," Phil said. "You look like you're gonna fold. It'll make you feel good."

"No, no more. I gotta go."

"Hey, come on, Kenny. I didn't tell you all that to make you feel bad. I don't blame you. I just wanted you to know."

"Yeah, okay. I'm glad you told me, but I gotta get out of here."

"You're right. Let's go. It's dark. The fireworks should be soon."

"I don't know. I think I better go home. I don't think I'll make it to the field."

"Don't sweat it, Kenny. I'm with you. You'll be fine once you get outside. The fireworks are going to be fantastic. I won't let you miss them."

I looked at Phil and laughed. He laughed, too. "The stoned leading the stoned," I said.

"Ah, but I'm a pro!" he exclaimed, and we walked out of the house arm in arm.

Chapter 24

Phil was right. I did feel better once we got outside; but still, walking was difficult. I felt like I was on an escalator going backward. Phil put on his old charm. I don't know if it was the pot or him, but we laughed ourselves silly to the field.

Once I saw the crowds of people, I panicked. "We're acting too stoned," I cried. "It's too obvious."

"Relax, Kenny. Half the kids here are probably turned on."

"You think so?"

"I know so. Don't they all look stoned?"

I looked around. Phil was right. Even the grandmothers and the grandfathers looked stoned.

"Amazing," I said.

"You wait right here. I'm going to find out when the fireworks start." Phil vanished into the throngs of people. After a couple of years he re-emerged. The show's not on for about an hour. But there's dancing and a band some place. Let's find it."

I followed Phil through the crowd and over to the dancing. The music sounded tremendous. It was bouncing off the sky and filtering back into my head like I was the only person in a giant concert hall.

"Do I feel like dancing!" I told Phil.

"Go on and ask someone. There are plenty of girls hanging around."

"I can't. I mean, I can't just go up and ask a girl to dance."

"Why not?" He grinned. "See that blonde with the big boobs?"

"Yeah."

"I'm gonna dance with her."

"You're kidding! You're going to walk over to a chick like that and you think she'll dance with you? She's gotta be at least eighteen."

"Watch this." He grinned again and made his way across the dance floor to her. He began talking and the next thing I knew they were dancing.

I looked around. There were a couple of likely candidates but I couldn't get up the nerve. So I stood there and watched Phil dance. When the music stopped he came over to me with the girl and another girl.

"Kenny, this is Cheryl and her friend Maryanne."

Maryanne smiled at me and I smiled back. I thought she was gorgeous.

"Kenny's shy," Phil went on. That's all he had time to say because the music started again. Maryanne and I began to dance. She was a great dancer. I kept on looking at her and wondering if she was stoned, too. I wasn't sure and I wasn't about to ask her. So we kept on dancing and smiling at each other. I smiled so much my jaw began hurting.

Suddenly Maryanne was gone. Like a dream, right in the middle of the dance, her friend Cheryl appeared and whooshed her away—without even saying goodbye.

"What's happened?" I asked Phil, and then I cried, "Now I know how Cinderella's prince felt at the strike of midnight."

"Stroke," Phil said.

"What?"

"It's the stroke of midnight."

"Oh. Anyway, what happened?"

"I don't know," he moaned. "There I was, kissing her neck and whispering sweet nothings in her ear . . ."

"No kidding," I said. "What went wrong?"

"I asked her if she wanted to smoke."

"And?"

"And she said no. Then she asked me what kind of a girl I thought she was. She said she didn't go out with potheads. So I pointed out that we had just met and that we weren't on a date. And she walked away."

"And took Maryanne with her." I felt like crying.

"I think I need some more," Phil said.

"Me, too. But not here."

"Come on, over there," he said, pointing to a bunch of trees.

Phil lit up and I had a couple of drags. My head began swimming.

"Better?" Phil asked.

"Much."

We went back to the dance. I spied Maryanne and I could tell she'd been looking at me. So I smiled and she turned away.

Phil began pulling at my shoulder. "Kenny! Look who's over there dancing. It's your old pal, The Mental!"

"Where? I don't believe it."

I followed Phil's finger and there he was—Harold in all his glory. "God, is he retarded!" I exclaimed.

"You just noticed?"

"I'm serious. I think he's gotten worse again. I mean it, Phil. I've seen him dance before. He used to be a good dancer."

"You've heard of rose-colored glasses?" Phil chuckled.

"Yeah, I guess you're right. Let's get closer. I bet you anything Rachel is with him."

We made our way through the crowd until we were only about ten feet away. I was right. Rachel was there. She was standing next to Kathy and two guys. One had his arm around Kathy. The other one was standing next to Rachel. I recognized him immediately. It was Carl. He wasn't touching Rachel but he was leering at her.

"Look at that creep," I said to Phil.

"Which one?"

"The one who's standing next to Rachel. Now tell me—is he leering at her or is it my imagination?"

"Leering like a lecher," Phil agreed. "Do you know him?"

"Rachel was with him this afternoon. I think he's a mental teacher."

"A teacher? I don't think so," Phil said. "He's not old enough."

"Neither is Rachel and she's teaching this summer."

"Oh."

Rachel and Carl began to dance.

"I can't believe Rachel is going out with him," I said, and felt like crying and punching the creep at the same time.

"Do you know that for a fact?" Phil asked.

I thought about it. "No, not for a fact," I admitted.

"So don't worry. Maybe they're just here as part of their mental job."

I thought about that. I looked at Carl. He was so preppy-looking I could have puked. He was tall, slim with a haircut that probably cost ten bucks, a Levi's shirt, and ironed jeans—not to mention a mustache.

"He's so preppy-looking I could puke," I said out loud.

Phil agreed. "Probably spends more time in front of the mirror in one day than you and I spend together all week."

I kept on looking at his mustache and rubbing the stupid fuzz above my upper lip.

"Maybe he just matured early," I said. "And then again maybe Rachel just dumped me for him—a preppy-looking creep."

Phil kept up a constant stream of derogatory remarks about "Carl the Preppy"—as we called him. I knew Phil was trying to make me feel better. But I didn't. I even stopped listening to him. I kept on staring at Rachel and Carl. There was no doubt about it, they were having a good time.

"I think I'm leaving," I told Phil.

"Come on, man. We haven't even seen the fireworks yet . . ."

"You stay. I just can't stand it anymore."

"But you're running, Kenny. That's been your whole problem with Rachel all along. When you think about it—she ran the show and you just ran."

"Yeah, you think so?"

"Definitely."

I thought what he said made sense, but when I thought more about it, I wasn't sure. I was having trouble keeping my thoughts straight again.

"I better go," I decided.

Phil grabbed hold of me and said, "Don't you see! By letting her run the show you were running away from your responsibility to yourself."

I couldn't argue with him. "What should I do?"

"I'm not sure, yet. But you can't run. Wait. I'll think of something."

While Phil was thinking I was getting more stoned. It was weird. I felt as though I'd just had a few more drags, but I hadn't. I couldn't take my eyes off Rachel and Carl the Preppy. No, Rachel and Harold! I began getting frightened. They were merging together.

They were dancing. They were standing together talking and laughing. Harold was holding her hand. She was holding his hand. He was hugging her. Maybe I was seeing things. God, was Harold ugly and retarded! I'd forgotten how retarded he was. Why couldn't he keep his hands off Rachel? What was she doing with a retardate anyway? What was she doing with someone like Carl? Rachel, Harold, and Carl the Preppy—Rachel, Harold, and me.

Carl took Rachel's hand. They were dancing. Harold was dancing, too. By himself. With them. With Rachel.

Harold and Rachel. Carl and Rachel. I felt like I was going to explode. What is going on! What is going on! I kept on screaming inside my head.

"Phil, I gotta go," I finally said. "I'm getting scared. This stuff is doing crazy things to my head."

"Be cool, Kenny. It'll pass."

"It won't," I insisted. "Every time I think it is, I get more stoned."

"Let's get a Coke. The refreshment stand is still open. My treat."

I let Phil lead me like a dog on a leash. But I didn't care. Anything to get away from Rachel and Harold and Carl.

There was a long line at the stand. The lights were glaring around it, bright and ugly. They lit up people's faces in a grotesque way. The other people didn't look stoned anymore. They just looked ugly. But the ugliest of all was Harold. He was standing across from me, grinning at me. Rachel was with him. He was holding her hand and grinning at me.

"I don't believe it," I said to Phil. "The Mental is standing right over there. I mean, look, Phil. Is he or isn't he?"

Phil looked. "He is."

"What a relief. I thought I was seeing things."

Phil laughed. "You don't hallucinate on grass, Kenny. I think maybe The Mental is following you."

Rachel had seen me, too. There was no doubt she had heard us. She looked so snotty and superior standing there. I was glad she'd heard us. I wanted her to hear us.

"But you know what is really gross, Phil?" I went on talking even louder. "What I think is really gross is the love and devotion mentals get from perfectly normal people."

"You got a point there, Kenny, old pal!" Phil laughed.

"And I think what's even worse, I mean, about the worst thing, is the way a perfectly normal girl goes out of her way to turn on a retard."

I was staring right at Rachel when I said that. She pretended not to hear, but I knew she had. Phil and I started laughing hysterically.

Rachel walked over to me and said, "I think you better shut up, Kenny."

"It's a free world, Rachel. I can say whatever I want. Nobody's making you stand here. But while you are standing here, I do have a question for you, which is: Just what kind of a turn-on is it for you to be around Harold?"

Rachel didn't say a word. Her face tightened. At first she looked shocked—then angry. I thought she was going to hit me.

I turned to Phil. "Actually, I find it somewhat insulting. I think she's more turned-on by The Mental than she was by me."

"Don't let it bother you," Phil consoled me. "It says more about her than you."

By this time Harold had joined our little group and was jumping nervously from one foot to another.

"I think you are the most disgusting person I've ever known," Rachel said.

I sighed. "Is that all? I expected a better come-back than that."

"Kenny, you be nice to Rachel. Be nice," Harold pleaded.

"Are you going to let a retard tell you what to do?" Phil laughed.

"Good point, Phil." I nodded to him and turned to Harold. "Keep your mouth shut, retard. One more word out of you . . ." I laughed and made a fist and pretended that I was going to punch him.

Harold pulled his head back and made this weird face that broke Phil and me up.

"Keep your hands to yourself!" Rachel screamed at me.

"What do you think? I was really gonna hit the retard?" I said to her, and then turned to Phil. "Rachel thought I was going to hit the retard!"

"I told you the retard's catching. And she's catching it." Phil laughed.

"Kenny!" Harold cried. "You and me friends. I like you!" And he held out his hand to me.

I pushed it away and said, "Yeah, you're just about the greatest pal I've ever had. And just for the record —I mean, just so we're absolutely clear on this matter of our friendship, retard, I want you to know that I think you're the ugliest, stupidest, most retarded retard I've ever known!"

"Good, Kenny, baby!" Phil shrieked. "I couldn't have done better myself."

"Thank you, thank you." I bowed to Rachel and Harold. "Thank you, one and all . . . for all the great times . . ."

"You're going to feel sorry for this!" Rachel threatened.

I laughed in her face. "Did you hear that, Phil? Rachel threatened me."

"I heard. I'll be your witness."

"I hate you, Kenny Shea!" she screamed, and lunged for me.

I caught her hands in midair, and Harold came clawing after me, crying, "I like you, Kenny. Be nice to Rachel."

I let go of Rachel and pushed Harold away. I didn't mean to knock him down, but he fell.

"Carl!" I heard Rachel scream.

I turned just in time to see Carl the Preppy heading at me. He looked fierce.

"Lay off, man!" I shouted.

That's when Carl hit me.

I thought I was going to pass out. He grabbed hold of me and threw me against the side of the refreshment stand. I felt myself crumbling to the ground in the most terrible pain I'd ever felt in my whole life. All the time I could hear Phil screaming out my name and pulling at me to get up. I could hear Harold, too. He was crying, "What I do, Kenny? I like you. You and me friends, Kenny."

Phil helped me up and I looked around for Harold. The whole world was going around in circles and Harold's face was right in the middle. I was scared. I was sinking. I needed something to hang on to, but all I could see was Harold . . .

"I like you, Kenny. You and me friends, Kenny. I like you."

. . . Stop pleading, Harold. I can't stand it any-more. I'm sinking and you're pleading! I didn't want to sink, so I screamed, "I don't like *you*, Harold! You're a retarded shitface!"

"Let's get out of here," Phil cried, and began pulling me. I started to run, but I could still hear Harold calling my name. It sounded like he was following me. And I could hear Rachel, too. She was calling after Harold.

Chapter 25

Somehow Phil got me home. I don't remember much. The world kept falling off at a ninety-degree angle and I kept falling with it. I have vague memories of having to say hello to my parents and some of their friends. I remember climbing up the stairs. I felt like I was going the wrong way on an escalator again. With a great effort I made it to my bed and collapsed.

When I woke up the next morning I felt fine except everything came back to me like a nightmare. I remembered every detail but I couldn't believe it. I couldn't believe I'd said those things to Rachel and Harold. I prayed it really hadn't all happened. Maybe I had just dreamed it or imagined it after all. I figured the only way to find out was to ask Phil.

I thought of going over to see him, but I called him instead. His house was last night and I didn't want to go back.

Phil answered the phone. "Kenny! How do you feel this morning?" he said happily.

"Okay . . ."

"So what do you think about smoking. Fantastic?"

"Yeah—I don't know. I mean, Phil, I gotta talk to you."

"Come on over. Perry's gone. We can sit and smoke and talk."

"No. I can't. I just want to know if all those things happened—with Harold and Rachel."

"Did they ever, Kenny, baby! And you were fantastic. Absolutely fantastic."

I felt sick. "I gotta go," I told him.

"You don't sound so good. Something wrong?"

"Hey, look, Phil. I can't talk now."

"I'll come over. You sound like you need someone."

"No. No—don't. I'm busy. I'm going out with my father."

"Yeah, sure." Phil laughed. "It's that chick, man. Reality? Remember?"

"I can't talk about it now, Phil. I gotta go. I'll see you," I said, and hung up.

I felt like throwing the phone across the room and me with it. God, how did this happen? Why did I ever go with Phil last night? Why? Why? I screamed to myself and kicked the wastepaper basket across the room instead.

How could I have called Harold out like that? Harold, a retard who only wanted to be my friend. I couldn't believe it. It was worse than anything Phil had ever done. I wanted to call Rachel. I wanted to tell her I was sorry. I didn't want her to think I'd degenerated to Phil's level. I picked up the phone at least five times to dial her number and each time I'd hang up. I couldn't make my fingers dial. What would I say to her? How could I explain it? My stomach was in knots and my head was pounding. I had to talk to her. I had to explain it. I'd tell her the truth. That's all.

I picked up the phone and dialed. It rang three

times. I was about to hang up when I heard Rachel's voice. "Hello," she said.

"Rachel. This is Kenny. I have to talk . . ."

She slammed down the phone.

It wasn't until two days later that the real repercussions of the Fourth of July hit. I'd just come back from my first day at work. My mother was sitting on the front porch like she was waiting for me. She had to be waiting for me because she never just sits on the front porch in the middle of the day. And she didn't look like she was enjoying it, either.

"I want to talk to you, Kenny," she said. It was more like an order. I knew it had to do with the Fourth. I followed her into the kitchen and we sat down. She looked at me for a few seconds without saying anything.

I couldn't stand the suspense any longer. "What is it?" I asked.

"A young lady named Kathy Fisher called me."

"Harold's teacher."

She nodded.

"She told you, I suppose."

"She told me a story that I find hard to believe, Kenny."

"Well, it's true!" I shouted. "It's all true. I punched out a retard and called him names."

"But why?"

"I can't explain it, Mom. I just can't. It happened."

"She said Rachel thought that you and Phil were drunk or high on marijuana."

"We weren't drunk. I swear."

"Were you high?" she demanded.

"God, no!" I screamed.

"You can tell me, Kenny. I'm not naïve. I know that drugs are around . . ."

"I already told you the answer. If you think I'm lying, I can't change your mind."

"Kenny, it's not just a matter of smoking or drinking. And I want to believe you. I know you don't lie to me. But this whole thing is so bizarre. It's not like you. It's like Phil maybe, but not you. I've been thinking and thinking about it all morning and I just can't make any sense out of it. Not after all the time you spent with Harold. Not after knowing you the way I do. At least if you were drunk or high, it would make a little sense, Kenny. But you and Phil together again —and your lashing out at Harold . . ."

"Don't go blaming Phil. It was my fault. All of it. That's all I can tell you, Mom. I'm sorry . . ."

"No, Kenny! Being sorry isn't enough. Harold ran after you and Phil that night. He got lost in the crowd and he hasn't been seen since."

"What?"

"He's been missing for three days. His poor mother is beside herself. Her husband is in the hospital with a stroke, and now this. God, Kenny. Why did you do it?"

I felt terrible. I felt terrible for Harold, for Mrs. Havermeyer and for my mother. She was so upset and I wanted to tell her, give her some explanation. But I couldn't. It didn't make sense to me. I could have told her I was stoned. I believed her when she said she wouldn't be so angry. I knew she would try to understand, but it wasn't just being stoned. I knew that. There was so much more I didn't know or understand. I wasn't sure about anything anymore except I wished I'd never met Phil that day and I wished I'd never smoked pot and I wished Harold was okay and I wished I still didn't love Rachel so much.

My mother squeezed my hands gently and said, "I've known something's been bothering you for days, Kenny. We've always been able to talk before. You can trust me and, whatever it is, we can work it out together. Sometimes it's impossible to go it alone."

"I know that, Mom."

"Is it your father? Are you afraid of what he'll say?"

"No, it's not that, either. Whatever he says or does I guess I deserve."

"Something's eating you up inside, Kenny. It'll be better if you talk about it."

"There's nothing to talk about, Mom. I did it. That's all."

"Oh, God, Kenny, I just pray they find that boy all right."

So did I.

Chapter 26

There was no word on Harold for four days. Then Felix called me.

"I thought you might want to know. The police found him," Felix said. He spoke softly and without emotion. I had to listen hard to hear him.

And then he didn't say anything. I waited. There was nothing but silence. It was my turn to speak. "Is he okay?" I managed to get out. It didn't sound like me speaking.

"We're not sure yet. He's in the hospital."

"What happened?"

"Nobody knows. He was found all beaten up in a condemned building in Melrose where junkies hang out."

Melrose is about fifty miles from Baldwin. "How did he get to Melrose?" I asked.

"How do I know?" Felix snapped.

I felt like my insides were coming out. "I'm sorry. I really am."

"Christ, Kenny!" he exploded. "Why'd you do it?" And then he sighed deeply like he was trying not to cry. "You of all people! What happened?"

"I don't know," I said softly. I wanted to say something else. I wanted to tell him. I wanted to give him a reason. Something. I couldn't. I sat there listening to his breathing.

He finally spoke again. "You gotta really hate him to treat him like that."

"I don't hate him."

"Then why, Kenny? Why? He loves you."

"I'm sorry."

There was another long silence and I wished Felix would just hang up on me.

"I don't know, I don't know," he sighed. "But you're the one who's got to live with it." He paused and then he shouted, "And I hope it makes you choke!"

I don't believe in hell, but if it exists it couldn't be worse than what I went through for the next few days. I felt like there was a knife in my gut and somebody was slowly turning it. Every time the phone rang I'd feel sick. I was sure it was someone calling to say that Harold had died or had totally freaked out and would never come out of it.

I was on a guilt trip like never before and I deserved it. The only thing that kept me going was the job. It was a place to go every day, something to do. I could forget everything when I was teaching those crazy little kids how to swim. Some of them were scared of the water and cried a lot. Some of them could hardly stand in the pool without it coming up to their necks, still they loved it and tried so hard. But the job was just for the morning. In the afternoon I had nothing to do. I'd come home and hide out in my room.

I couldn't even look at my mother. Maybe she felt worse than me. My father had yelled and carried on and gotten it over with, but my mother just looked sad and hurt. And sometimes I thought that if she would just hold me like I was a kid and tell me everything would be all right, then it would be. But it wasn't so easy. She kept on bugging me about calling Mrs. Havermeyer and talking to her or going over to see her.

"I can't do that, Mom," I told her. "I just can't make myself do it."

"It's the very least you owe the woman."

Finally I promised I'd call. I didn't, but I told my mother I had. I guess she didn't believe me because one day when I came home from work she told me, "I'm going over to see Mrs. Havermeyer this afternoon. I think you should come, too."

I thought about it. I knew she was right. I knew I should go to see her, but I couldn't. I just couldn't. Instead, I sat in my room the whole time she was at the Havermeyers' wishing I could have gone with her— telling myself I should have gone and in general doing a whole number on my head.

I heard my mother come home, but I didn't go downstairs. I was waiting for her to come to me. She didn't, so I finally went to her.

"How is she?" I asked my mother.

"She's a strong woman, Kenny. She invited me in and insisted I have coffee and cake with her. We sat and talked. She talked about you and Harold and Rachel. She told me how much Harold loves you and how wonderful you were to him. She doesn't hate you or even blame you. She's just confused and hurt. We all are."

"Did she say how Harold is? Will he be okay?"

"He was badly beaten. But he'll be okay."

I felt so relieved to hear Harold was okay, I almost cried.

Phil called about a half-hour later. That was all I needed. He'd been calling me every day, wanting to get together. Every day I gave him another excuse. Today I couldn't think of any so I said, "Look Phil, I just don't want to see you or anybody. I'm depressed. I want to be alone."

"You shouldn't be alone in your state. I'm coming over."

"Don't . . ." I began, but he'd hung up. I thought of leaving, of just not being home when he came; but I figured that sooner or later I'd have to confront him.

About fifteen minutes later he appeared in my room. I hadn't heard him come in.

"How's it going?" He grinned and sat down on my bed.

"It's been better."

"Wow, I get the feeling I'm not wanted around here. First your mother treats me like I'm Dracula and you're not much better."

"I told you, Phil. I want to be alone."

"It's The Mental, huh? Getting beat up and all."

"How'd you know?"

"Word gets around."

"You get any flak?"

"Nah, not much. It seems everyone blames you."

"Yeah, well, I guess that's something."

"Look, Kenny, I don't see why you gotta blame

yourself like this. A mental runs off and gets mixed up with a bunch of creeps who work him over. It's tough, but it could have happened any time. He could just have been walking down the street and those creeps could of picked him up and done the same thing. Don't you see?"

"It could have. But it didn't."

"I know what you need!" he grinned, pulling two joints out of his pocket.

"You gotta be kidding!"

"Well, not here. Let's split somewhere."

"Not in the mood."

"That's ridiculous! How can you not be in the mood to smoke? Come on," he insisted, pulling me off the bed. "It'll do you good. Make you forget your problems."

"I don't think so. The last time it only made problems."

"You gotta forget that. It wasn't your fault. You gotta listen to your old friend, Kenny."

"I'm sorry, Phil. I can't buy that."

"All right, don't! But does that mean you're never gonna smoke again?"

"Look, Phil, I don't know. Right now I don't care about smoking. Would you just stop pushing me!"

"Okay, okay, man! I just came over to help," he said, and started to leave. When he got to the door, he turned around and said, by way of apology I guess, "If you don't want to smoke it's okay with me. We can just go out and ride the bikes."

There was something sad about Phil, standing there as he was. Sad and even a little desperate—more desperate than me, Harold, or Rachel. I knew he needed me, but I couldn't help him. How could I help anyone else if I couldn't even get my own head together?

"Another time, Phil. I gotta be alone now. I just have to be alone."

To top the day off, Felix called me that night. Would I mind going to see Harold? Harold had been asking for me. No, I wouldn't mind going to see him at all. That's what I told Felix. What else could I say?

Felix picked me up at two the next afternoon. It took almost an hour to drive to the hospital. I don't think he said one word to me the whole time. I tried to start a conversation. Maybe if we could have talked, maybe I could have tried to explain it to him—even a little. I wish I could have. It bothered me that Felix thought I was the scum of the earth. But he made it clear he didn't want to talk.

I followed Felix from the parking lot through the hospital like a shadow. I don't like hospitals. I've been an all-too-frequent visitor: first because of appendicitis, then a kid once stuck a pencil in my eye, and I've broken my leg once and my arm twice. I guess I used to be what is called accident prone. But it all stopped when I was about ten. I hadn't been in a hospital since.

But even scarier than my memories was the thought of Harold. I had no idea what to expect. I'd never seen someone who'd been beaten up before. I tried to envision the worst and that just about made it.

"How you doing, Harold?" Felix called as he opened

the door. Harold had been facing the other way but he jerked around when he heard Felix. I couldn't believe my eyes. He looked like he'd been through a masher. His face was so badly swollen I could hardly recognize him and where it wasn't swollen it was black and blue. His arm was in a cast.

"Hi, Kenny!" he shouted as soon as he saw me. I couldn't believe he could see anything out of his eyes.

"Hi, Harold, how you doing?"

"Go on over," Felix whispered to me.

I stood next to the bed. Harold was just grinning at me like nothing had happened. He reached out to shake my hand, and then he said, "I'm sorry, Kenny. You still my friend?"

I tried to speak but there was a lump in my throat the size of a tomato. It was all I could do not to start crying right there. Here I had called him every name I could think of, punched him out and been responsible for God knows what—and all he cared about was if I was still his friend.

When I didn't answer, he became a little frantic. "I like you, Kenny. You my friend?"

"Yeah," I said, and my voice cracked. "I'm your friend. Here, I brought you something." I gave him a bunch of comic books. He loves comics.

"Thanks, Kenny!" he shouted. "I'm glad you my friend."

I couldn't stop the tears. Harold didn't notice. He was too busy looking at the comics. I walked over to the window and tried to get control. A box of tissues came plummeting through the air.

"Blow your nose," Felix ordered.

I looked at Felix. "I'm sorry. I'm sorry."

"It's too late for sorry, Kenny."

"Felix, please . . ."

"You know something, Kenny? After I leave you off today—nothing would make me happier than never to see you again."

Chapter 27

I didn't see Harold or Felix or Rachel for the rest of the summer. I wasn't even sure what had happened to Harold. I knew he didn't come home again. Mr. Havermeyer came home at the end of July. He was in a wheelchair and he looked like he was in pretty bad shape. Sometimes I'd see him sitting on the porch all by himself. He'd always wave to me and smile, so I'd wave back. I guess nobody told him what I'd done to Harold. Still, I always passed the Havermeyers' house with caution. I didn't want to meet Mrs. Havermeyer. And once, when I saw Felix's car parked in front of the house, I walked the long way home. There was no way I could face meeting him.

I don't know how I would have gotten through the summer if it wasn't for the swimming job. I had to be there by eight-forty-five and every forty-five minutes there was another class of kids until twelve-thirty. I had wanted to teach the intermediate and life-saving classes, but because this was my first year, I had to teach the beginners, mostly six through eight years old.

At first I thought it would be a drag, but it turned out I liked teaching these kids. I guess I'd figured that they'd all be either pains in the neck or total nonentities—younger versions of my sister and her friends—but they weren't, at least not most of them.

There was this one little kid in particular who got to me. His name was Michael Skinner I learned later and he was six years old. We became buddies. He was more scared than any of the other kids. His mother practically had to drag him to the pool. On the first day, the other kids gathered together in one place, without their mothers; but Michael refused to let his mother go. He stood next to her, clutching her arm. His lips were quivering and the tears were gushing from his eyes. He wasn't making a sound. I really felt for him. I'd never seen a kid look so scared.

"Looks like one of yours," Steve Miller, the head instructor, said to me, chuckling.

"Yeah," I sighed.

"See if you can get rid of the mother. It's always easier without them."

The mother looked relieved as I headed in her direction. "I'm sorry," she apologized. "But he's very frightened."

"I can see that," I said. "It might be better if you left."

"No! I want to go home!" Michael screamed.

His mother tried to pry Michael loose, but he was hanging on for dear life. "Maybe I'd better take him home," she sighed.

"No, he'll be all right," I promised. "It'll be better if you leave."

"You heard what the teacher said," Mrs. Skinner said firmly to Michael. "I have to go now."

I guess Michael understood that he had no choice because he let me take him. He transferred his ferocious grasp to me and stood staring after his mother until she was out of sight. Then I bent down to Michael's level and said, "Hi. What's your name?"

He stared at me for a few seconds, and with the tears still coming, he managed to say, "Michael."

"Well, hi, Michael. My name's Kenneth, but everybody calls me Kenny. What does everybody call you? Mike?"

He shook his head.

"Mikey?"

He shook his head.

"Michael?"

He gave me a mournful nod.

"Okay, Michael it is. Have you ever been in a big pool like this before?"

Again, silently, he shook his head.

There was nothing I could do to get Michael to come near the pool, much less put in even his feet. For the first three days he stood in the corner, clutching his towel and staring. After a while I realized he was staring at me, watching me, never taking his eyes off me. He didn't cry. He just stared. So I began looking back at him. At first I'd just look and smile. Every so often I'd get a glimmer of a smile back from him. Then I began making funny faces at him. At first he'd look away. Then he began smiling. Finally, on the fourth day, he laughed and made a funny face back at me. The next day he didn't stand in the corner. Slowly he began inching his way over toward the edge of the pool. When he came in on Friday, he walked over to the edge with the rest of the kids and sat down with his feet in the water. He still hadn't said a word to me except his name.

Michael sat at the edge of the pool all during the class, kicking the water with his feet and making faces at me. Every time I'd ask him if he was ready to come in, he'd shake his head. When the class was over, one little girl named Marissa, who loved getting my attention, went over to Michael and said, "I hope you come in the water soon."

While the other kids were gettting their towels and leaving, Michael sat at the edge of the pool.

"It's time to go now," I told him.

He looked at me for a few seconds and finally spoke. "If you hold me, I'll go in, Kenny."

How could I refuse? I picked him up and he wrapped his arms around my neck with the grasp of a drowning man. I walked around in the water for a few minutes and then he said, "I have to go now."

I put him up on the edge of the pool and he said to me in a deep, flat voice, "I have a dog named Taffy. A rabbit and a guinea pig and a lizard named Nosy."

"Hey, no kidding!" I smiled.

"I'll see you tomorrow, Kenny."

"Not tomorrow. Tomorrow's Saturday. I'll see you Monday."

"How many days is that?" he asked.

"Two."

"I wish it was tomorrow," he said sadly, got his towel, and began to leave.

"See ya Monday, Michael," I called.

"See ya Monday, Kenny!" He smiled and ran to the dressing room.

"I thought that kid didn't know how to talk," Steve Miller said to me. "He sure is a strange one."

"I like him. He'll be okay."

On Monday Michael came in with a big grin on his face. He hurried over to me and said, "My guinea pig had two babies yesterday." And he sat down at the edge of the pool.

Michael's was the last class of the day, so when he stayed to talk to me I didn't mind. I began to look forward to it. He knew a lot about animals and insects and he loved to unload all his knowledge on me. He'd give me a progress report on his guinea pig babies or tell me how many grasshoppers or butterflies he'd caught the day before. He had a strange way of talking, as if there were no such things as commas or periods in the English language. He'd just talk on and on, in his flat, sagelike voice until he'd finished whatever it was he'd planned to tell me.

It took Michael almost another week before he'd go into the water alone, but after that he was okay.

One day he brought me a praying mantis he'd caught. He showed it to me before class and after class he gave it to me. "I caught it for you, Kenny. Praying mantises make good pets. I let them crawl all over me so they get to know my smell. Then they stay with me. See," he said, taking the praying mantis out of the jar and letting it crawl on his arms and neck and back. Then it was my turn. I pretended to be scared and Michael laughed and laughed.

"Do you have an old fish tank or something?" he asked.

"I think so."

"If you put him in it, with twigs and grass and catch

grasshoppers for him, he might live all summer and make an egg."

And then, as if Michael wasn't sure I knew how to catch insects, he'd come in every morning after that with a grasshopper or moth in a little bag for me to take home and feed to my praying mantis. I followed Michael's directions and set up the praying mantis in the fish tank on the same shelf where I still kept a picture of Rachel.

The swimming classes were over by the time the mantis laid its egg, but I got Michael's phone number and called him to tell him.

"My praying mantis laid an egg, too," he told me, and then went on in his serious, knowing voice, "and if you keep it all winter, in the spring the egg will hatch and hundreds of babies will come out. Except most of them eat each other."

"I'll keep it," I promised.

Chapter 28

In some crazy way, Michael Skinner made everything with Harold and Rachel and Felix a little less painful. But for a long time I couldn't think about what had happened with Harold without feeling guilt and pain. I wasn't sure what hurt most—losing Rachel or what I'd done to Harold and even Felix. The thought of a guy like Felix hating my guts was hard to take.

Phil was also a problem. He kept on calling me. I think he was usually stoned when he called. I didn't know how to put him off. Once or twice I even agreed to meet him and then at the last minute I'd call back with an excuse.

One afternoon he was waiting for me when I got off from work. He looked terrible. He had a black eye and his nose was swollen.

"What happened to you?" I asked.

"Perry," he said, as if it hurt to talk.

"Perry! What'd he do that for?"

"The grass. He found out I was taking his grass."

"I thought he knew."

He laughed bitterly and shook his head. "Unfortunately I was sitting behind the garage, stoned, numb to the world, when he came looking for me. He saw me and came at me like a rabid dog."

"How'd he know you were taking his grass?"

"He asked me before he smeared me against the side of the garage. Like a fool I admitted it. I was so stoned it didn't seem to matter."

"I'm sorry."

"No sorrier than I am, man. I don't know where to get the stuff now. And besides, Perry says it goes for twenty bucks an ounce. At that rate he figures I owe him a couple of hundred bucks."

"What are you going to do?"

"Nothing. Screw him. I'm not paying him a penny."

Phil and I spent the afternoon together. It was a total disaster. He was bitter and sarcastic, not to mention depressed. I couldn't take being with him and I guess he sensed it. He finally left, accusing me of being boring and condescending. I didn't try to stop him. I didn't hear from him for the rest of the summer.

My job ended in the middle of August and luckily I got a letter from the coach saying that on August 19 he was starting football practice three afternoons a week. There was a terrible heat wave at the end of the month. The temperature stayed about ninety-five degrees for almost two weeks, but I didn't miss a practice. One day, when I was at the bottom of a gigantic pile-up of bodies on the twenty-five-yard line, I made a decision: for the next two years I was going to do only two things—play football and study. If I never went out on a date with a girl, I wouldn't care.

Having made that decision, I started school with great expectations. As far as I was concerned, there was no place for me to go but up. Mind over matter, I figured. Nothing was going to stop me. That's what

I kept on telling myself anyway. I thought if I told myself that enough times I'd believe it.

But the very first class of the year proved that matter has the ultimate power over the mind. It was English and I was late because of a schedule mix-up. The teacher was just assigning seats, alphabetically.

"Shea," I said. "Kenneth Shea."

"Good." She smiled. "I'm just up to the S's. Anthony Santiago. And then you, Kenneth. You sit behind Anthony. Let's see. Rachel Simon, you sit behind Kenneth."

My stomach dropped. I hadn't noticed Rachel as I'd hurried in and here she was, walking down the aisle behind me. I stopped at my desk and turned to her. "Some coincidence!" I smiled.

She didn't smile. All she said was "Yeah." And sat down.

The class lasted forever. I couldn't concentrate on anything except the fact that Rachel was sitting behind me. I couldn't stop my heart from thudding like crazy. As soon as the bell rang, I jumped up. I hadn't planned to. It was an involuntary reflex. I turned to Rachel and said, "What's your next class?"

"French."

"No kidding. That's mine, too. Room 301?"

She looked at her schedule and nodded. I looked at her schedule and said, "Hey look at this! We have math and a study hall together, too."

"Lucky me," she said, and left.

I couldn't believe she hated me as much as she seemed to. So I made a point of talking to her as often as I could, which wasn't too hard considering we had four classes together. Persistence, I told myself.

One morning when I was walking with her between English and French, talking about nothing in particular, she stopped and looked me straight in the eye.

"I have something very important to tell you, Kenny. You are annoying me. Bothering me. I have nothing to say to you and I wish you wouldn't follow me from class to class like this. Is that clear enough? I can't think of any other way to put it."

She sounded and looked so snobby, I laughed.

"I'm glad you find that so amusing," she said angrily.

"I'm glad you find that so amusing," I mimicked her. "My, aren't we getting fancy lately."

She looked like she was ready to punch me. I liked her when she looked like that. Snobbiness wasn't her style.

"Let me put it this way, Kenny. I can't stand your guts. You're stupid and immature."

"And I suppose all your friends who teach retards are brilliant and mature."

"As a matter of fact, they are."

"Especially Carl," I said carelessly. I had no idea whether or not she and Carl the Preppy were going out, but from the look on her face I knew I'd hit a nerve.

She glared at me and said, "Yes, especially Carl."

"I didn't think he was your type."

"Well, he is. I'm sick of stupid, immature, slobby high school boys."

I felt like smearing mud all over her face. Instead, I

laughed and said, "Now I understand. Carl is a college man. My my, isn't Rachel getting up in the world. Not much I can do to compete with a preppy college man—especially one that goes in for retards."

"At least he's mature enough not to take out his frustrations and inadequacies on a retarded boy." And she turned and hurried down the hall.

There's nothing like being put down in no uncertain terms to make you want to crawl into a hole and die. But after a few days that feeling passed, and I began to get mad. Mad at myself for acting like a fool, and mad at Rachel, too. I'm not exactly sure why. Maybe it was because she succeeded in making me look so dumb. And maybe it was because I had given her the chance to make up—I had humbled myself, groveled at her feet—and still she had said no.

But that's okay, Rachel! I thought. Because I don't care anymore! I really don't care! You can stay with your retardates and your preppies! I couldn't care less!!!

Chapter 29

I hardly ever saw Phil in school. He cut half his classes and spent the other half spreading super-stud rumors about himself. Every time I ran into him he had that stoned, glassy-eyed look. I figured he'd found a new source. Then at the end of October he was suspended for smoking grass on campus. The first day he came back he asked me if I wanted to buy a couple of joints. He'd sell them to me cheap, for old times' sake.

"Phil, are you insane? What are you selling the stuff for? Christ, if you ever get caught . . ."

"Kicks, man. It's a trip selling the stuff. I'm just waiting for a teacher to try and buy some. Man, I'll triple the price. Which brings me to the second reason for selling—money. Where else can you make bread so easy?" He laughed.

"Come on, Phil. Let's talk about it. I mean smoking is one thing. But selling it . . ."

"Look, since you and me were once pals and all that crap, I'll give you a freebie."

"No, thanks anyway . . ."

"Oh! I forgot—our All-American boy here is in training. I know football stars are supposed to be heroes and all that. You'll pardon me if I don't bow."

"Oh, man," I sighed. We were worlds apart.

Phil took out a joint and lit up. We were in the basement stairwell, just outside the boys' locker room.

"Hey, come on, Phil. Not here."

He inhaled deeply and grinned.

As I climbed the stairs I could smell the grass and hear him laughing.

My life seemed to even out for a while after that. The football season was fantastic. I played every game and practiced as hard as I could. And besides the football, I ended up with an 88 average for the first marking period. That pleased my father.

I didn't have any close friends, but there were plenty of guys I goofed around with. That was all I needed or wanted. I stayed clear of parties and girls in general. I hardly saw Rachel. Of course we had those classes together, but after a while I almost forgot she was there. That's why I was really surprised when she tapped me on the shoulder at the beginning of English one morning and said, "I have to talk to you."

"About what?" I asked coolly.

"It's important, Kenny. Can you meet me at lunch?"

"I'm meeting someone," I said, which was a lie.

"It won't take long. It's just something I can't whisper in two seconds."

I guess it was the tone of her voice that made me say yes. She wasn't being nasty or antagonistic. She was sad.

Rachel was waiting for me outside the cafeteria.

"Hi, Kenny," she called.

"Hi. Hey, look, I have to make this fast . . ."

"It'll just take a minute. It's just something I thought you might want to know," she said softly. Suddenly her eyes filled with tears. She sighed deeply.

Instinctively I put my arm around her. She didn't pull away. Instead we moved over toward the corner.

When she looked at me again she was really crying. "Oh, Kenny," she half-whispered. "It's Mr. Havermeyer. He died yesterday. He had another stroke and died."

I heard her words but they didn't make any sense at first. Mr. Havermeyer dead. I hadn't thought about Mr. Havermeyer for months and in a moment I found myself remembering so many things about him: like the time he'd run after us when we went bowling, and how he'd insisted I take the five dollars; I thought of how he used to talk to Harold and how hard he'd tried to make Felix's wife smile last Christmas. It was hard to imagine him dead. I'd never known anyone who'd died before. I felt strange, sad and creepy at the same time.

"It's so terrible," I said to Rachel. "I liked him a lot."

"Me, too," she sighed.

We didn't say anything for a few moments. I didn't know what to say. We stood there, Rachel holding on to me and trying to stop crying.

Finally I said, "How's Harold?"

"I talked to Felix. He said Harold took it pretty well."

It was weird hearing Rachel talking about Harold

again—like old times, like everything bad that had happened had never happened and we were just standing there talking about Harold. Somehow that seemed much more real than Mr. Havermeyer's death.

"You see him much?" I asked.

Rachel let go of me on the pretext of getting a tissue from her bag. When she looked at me again, I knew the crisis had passed. She looked nervous, like she wanted to leave. But she didn't. She stared at me and then said, "I don't see him much. He's living in a foster home near his school."

"No kidding. You mean someone just took him in?"

"Will wonders never cease?" she sneered. "There are other queers besides me who have feelings for retardates . . ."

"Hey, I'm sorry. I didn't mean it the way it came out. I mean—I didn't know. I didn't even know when he got out of the hospital. I didn't even know there were foster homes like that."

"Okay—forgiven." She smiled. "You see, Felix knew that it would be impossible for his mother to take care of her husband and Harold, so he talked to the school and they found this nice place for Harold."

"I can't believe Mrs. Havermeyer let him go."

"God, she was so upset. But she didn't have much choice. Mr. Havermeyer was half-paralyzed and, besides, it's a great set-up for Harold. There are four other retarded boys living there with this couple who act like house parents. Harold takes care of himself completely. He's so happy."

"That's great. I mean, he could have ended up back in an institution."

"Would that have mattered to you?"

I thought for a second and said, "Yes. It would have mattered."

Rachel wrapped her arms around her books and squeezed them hard. She took a deep breath and said, "What happened that day. Why did you do it?"

"I don't know. It's complicated. I don't think I even understand it all."

"Maybe we can talk about it someday."

"I don't think so, but maybe we can talk someday."

"Yeah," she smiled. "I'd like that."

My heart began thudding so hard I felt it in my throat. We both got embarrassed and I thought she was going to make a fast exit. I didn't want her to leave. There was something else to say.

"Hey, Rachel, do you realize it's almost exactly a year since we took Harold bowling?"

She smiled. "Hey, remember that?"

I remembered. I'll always remember.

"You know something, Kenny? In the end it all worked out. I mean, Harold could have ended up back in an institution if it wasn't for us. God, it's mind-blowing when you think about it—because no matter what, Mr. Havermeyer would have had that stroke. If it wasn't for us, Harold could never have gotten into the place where he's living now."

I smiled and remembered: "The Socialization of Harold Havermeyer."

"It was important, Kenny. It was like saving a drowning person. He's so independent now, you wouldn't believe it. Kathy thinks that in a few years he may even be able to leave the school and get a paying job in one of those sheltered workshops for the handicapped."

"That's nice. It really is. Are you still working at Harold's school?"

"Not much. Just some Saturday afternoons."

Then we were silent. We looked at each other and I thought, there really is nothing more to say.

I guess we both knew it, but still we stood there looking at each other, half-smiling nervously, each waiting for the other to say goodbye.

Finally I said, "Thanks for letting me know, Rachel. And I'm sorry. I really am."

She smiled at me sadly and sighed. "I know that now. Me, too."

I turned to leave and Rachel called me back. "Kenny, Mrs. Havermeyer is really taking it hard. She's all alone. She always asks me how you are."

I stared at Rachel for a few seconds. "Well, maybe I'll stop in and see her."

"She'd like that, Kenny. It'd mean a lot to her."

I didn't have any plans for going to see Mrs. Havermeyer. I'd said that for Rachel. I knew it was what she wanted me to say. I didn't give Mrs. Havermeyer any more thought then. Instead I thought about Rachel and her smile—Rachel and me. Talking to her like that stirred up old memories, but the memories were painful. They were too mixed up with Felix and Harold and now Mr. Havermeyer's death.

Death—dying: it's a subject I find difficult to handle. I tried not to think about Mr. Havermeyer, but he kept on creeping into my mind all afternoon; when I least expected it, I'd remember something he'd said or the way he looked. I found myself wishing I'd been nicer to him, more friendly to him as he sat on the porch all summer, alone, waiting to die.

I couldn't shake the ghost of Mr. Havermeyer until football practice. I practiced like crazy, exercising and running, concentrating on everything I was doing as if we were playing a championship game. And I felt better afterward. Then, without ever making a conscious decision to go, I found myself walking up the Havermeyers' front walk on the way home from school.

Mrs. Havermeyer probably isn't even home, I told myself as I rang the bell. My stomach sank when I heard her footsteps.

"Who's there?" she asked.

"Kenny," I said, and my voice cracked. "Kenny Shea."

I heard her fumbling frantically with the latch. "Kenny!" she cried, as she opened the door. "Come in. Come in."

She looked old and tired. Her eyes were swollen from crying and her hair was loose and uncombed. "I heard about Mr. Havermeyer," I said. "I'm sorry. I liked him."

She shook her head and her eyes filled with tears. She took me by the arm and ushered me into the kitchen. "Some milk and cookies maybe?" she asked. "Like old times?"

"No. I don't want to bother you."

"Bother! What bother? Who do I have to bother about now?" And she began getting the milk and cookies. She set them before me and then sat down at the table. She looked across at me. I wanted to look away, but I could tell she was getting happier just looking. Finally she said, "So, Kenny, I'm so happy you're here. Happy? That sounds strange, I guess. How can I be happy now? He was old and sick and we bickered all the time. Even to the end we bickered. But forty-one years—that's a long time to live with someone."

I nodded, not knowing what to say. I glanced at Mrs. Havermeyer. She was looking past me, into the living room where Mr. Havermeyer used to sit and read his paper. Suddenly she began talking again. "So, did you hear about my Harold? He's living by himself now."

I nodded. "Rachel told me."

"It's wonderful. More than I could ever have hoped for. Of course I would like him here with me now, but Felix told me that would be wrong. He said Harold needs his independence." She stopped for a minute and sighed, and began to cry a little. "He's right, of course. I know that. But I miss my boy . . ." and then she couldn't go on.

I nibbled on the edge of a cookie.

Finally she began again, "I'm sorry, Kenny. It's so hard. Everything."

"I understand, Mrs. Havermeyer. If you want to be alone . . ."

She reached across the table and put her hand on mine as if to keep me there. "No, Kenny. Stay awhile. Felix will be here soon. Maybe he'd like to see you."

"I don't think so."

"Felix! His bark is so much worse than his bite. I know how he says he feels about you. But I know differently, Kenny. I know you're a good boy. I know you didn't mean to hurt Harold."

"I'm sorry. I'm so sorry. I wanted to tell you that before . . ."

"Enough. Let's not talk about it anymore. It's over. There was more good than bad—so much more."

"I better go now."

"Stay. Stay for a few minutes and see Felix," she pleaded.

I looked at her then. I wished she was right. I wished Felix would want to see me. But I knew she was wrong.

"It's late. I better go. My mother is waiting for me," I told her. "Maybe another time."

"Yes, another time," she sighed. And then she smiled. "That's a promise. You've stayed away too long. You come and see me."

"I will."

She walked me to the door and as I was about to leave she put her arms around me and squeezed me hard. "Oh, Kenny . . ." she sighed, still holding me. But she didn't go on. She let go and we looked at each other. She smiled sadly, as if she wanted to say something else. I waited, but all she said was, "Go. Hurry. Your mother is waiting."

It was almost dark when I left Mrs. Havermeyer. Dark, cold, and windy. I zipped up my jacket and pulled my hat out of my pocket—the hat the Havermeyers had given me for Christmas. I began walking, not home, not anywhere in particular. I just wanted to be alone.

I walked for a long time, thinking and remembering. But this time the memories weren't painful. If Mrs. Havermeyer could remember the good times then I could, too.

I was glad I'd gone to see her. I was glad that Rachel and I had talked. It meant something that they knew I was sorry. It wasn't earth-shattering, but it was enough. Besides, maybe in the end Rachel was right. Maybe what really mattered was that life was better for Harold. Rachel and I had shared something very special because of that—and maybe, in the end, that's what mattered most.

About the Author

Emily Hanlon has experience teaching retarded teen-agers in New York City. She is the author of two pic-turebooks, *What If a Lion Eats Me and I Fall into a Hippopotamus' Mud Hole?* and *How a Horse Grew Hoarse on the Site Where He Sighted a Bare Bear,* and is presently working on a second novel.

She lives with her husband and two children in York-town Heights, New York.